JASON DYE

228 Hamilton Ave.,
Palo Alto, CA 94301

ISBN 978-1-960946-29-4 (softcover)
ISBN 978-1-960946-28-7 (ebook)

This book is a work of fiction. Names, characters, places, and incidents are the product of the author's imagination or are used fictitiously. Any resemblance to actual locales, events, or persons, living or dead, is purely coincidental.

Printed in the United States of America.

To my loving wife:
Thank you for your understanding, support, and
encouragement. None of this would be possible without you

To my children:
Thank you for believing in me. Thank you for being
you and inspiring me to be the best version of myself.

To my friends, family, and fans:
Thank you for your support. I am
honored to earn your recognition.

PROLOGUE

In the not-so-distant future, life as we know it will disappear. In a few decades humans will be responsible for the decimation of most of the Earth's natural resources. Greed and entitlement plague humanity and devastate the natural evolution of the Earth.

Instead of conserving the remaining resources, humans use them to make weaponry and defend the remaining scarcities. Individualism replaces community. The scarcity of resources turns one against another, friend against friend, and family against family, state by state, territory by territory, and country by country. Wars rage, loyalties fade, armies implode, and basic social structures collapse.

A dramatic shift in the Earth's atmosphere creates devastating seasonal changes. Hurricanes and monsoons flood coastal cities and towns. Tornadoes rip up crops and level homes across the prairies and inlands. Earthquakes demolish entire cities. Volcanos fill the skies with toxic gases and cloud the sun. It is as if the planet is just as angry with humanity as humanity is with itself. Seasons change; spring and fall all but disappear. Winter and summer become extremely polarized, with temperatures too intense to sustain life. The climate on the surface of the planet becomes too unstable and harsh. People have no choice but to go underground.

Disease and famine then set in. Within a few years the population of the world falls less than 100 million. Civilization appears to be headed for extinction as death rates surpass sustainable births. The critical need for new energy sources is the only hope of reversing the trajectory toward the end of our species.

An alliance is formed on the precipice of the end of civilization. It is established with good intention: to restore order, provide structure, and reestablish societal constructs. A unified world government is created to help rebuild and recover. The agreed-upon primary language becomes Latin. Security forces are created, leaders take office, and laws are passed.

Exploration deeper into the Earth's core creates new opportunities for growth and discovery. During this exploration, two new elements are discovered.

The first to be found is discovered deep beneath magma channels. It has a natural red appearance and can be broken down and stabilized in all three states of matter. It is the most impenetrable of the metals and lightest in weight as a solid.

In its solid state, It has an unmistakable dark red-black color. As a gas it is a super conductor, capable of transferring enormous loads of energy, glowing more radiantly red the higher the energy transfer. In a liquid state it can store energy more efficiently and longer than lithium, as a thick, dark-red syrup.

This super element becomes heavily researched and tested as its capabilities far exceed anything found to date. It is named visium, after the Latin word *vis*, for strength and power.

The second new element to be found is named vigorium, named from the Latin word *vigor*, for its energy and vitality. It is found at the deepest parts of the world's oceans. It has a natural blue tint and can also be stabilized in each state of matter.

Vigorium is not as strong as visium when in its solid state and is penetrable only by visium. It is also super conductor and can store and transmit energy at a much higher rate and capacity than visium. When gaseous, vigorium glows a bright blue. As a liquid it is a royal blue with a higher viscosity than its counterpart. Research begins on this new super element as well.

The discoveries of these elements become a pivotal turning point for civilization. Clothing is created that can withstand the extreme temperatures on Earth's surface. Filters are created that purify the air and water to reduce the devastating carbon footprint that has been left. The economy begins to flourish as mining, processing, and manufacturing of these elements increase.

Power grids and communication systems are restored. People begin resurfacing and building small communities. Plant life begins to sprout. Individual and public transit are produced. Things appear to be heading back in a positive direction. Because of these changes, a few decades of peace pass as humankind pulls together.

The lust for power grows in the few remaining wealthy elite, for they control the resources. Another alliance is formed within these privileged few under the name of Imperium Corporation. The Imperium Corporation creates a monopoly of its own, controlling every other business that spawned from the discovery of these two hidden treasures.

Imperium demands more and more from the world government to further line their pockets. Inflation skyrockets, making costs unaffordable for most. The gap widens between the wealthy few and the remaining poor. Exploitation forces loyalty. Necessities become rationed in exchange for grueling labor.

Imperium builds its own army of soldiers and becomes less transparent regarding its research of the precious elements. The tension between the world government and Imperium grows. War eventually ensues. People flee for shelter as the weapons created from these elements are more powerful and destructive than ever before.

The government's army infiltrates Imperium Laboratories and fully extracts the research and data on vigorium. World government armies gain control of the vigorium mines. A clear dividing line is drawn. Unfortunately for the world government, the visium mines far exceed the vigorium mines in number and capacity. Within a few short years, the vigorium mines are all but depleted. The world government falls to Imperium in the bloodiest of battles, making Imperium the entity for law and order.

Those within the government army and loyal to its cause become a resistance force known as Initium Novum, Latin for *New Beginnings*. They harness the power of vigorium and use it in attempts to overthrow Imperium. Up to this point, all their attempts have failed.

CAPITULUM I
(CHAPTER 1)

The sun was setting as Joe walked south down an abandoned I-35 toward Des Moines. The trees were greener and fuller than he had ever seen them before, or at least more than he had ever noticed. The remains of abandoned vehicles were peppered up and down the deserted highway that was slowly being consumed by overgrowth. Weeds crawled across the pavement and seeped through the cracks in the road like a web of diseased veins.

Joe looked as alive and healthy as a slightly warmed corpse as he wearily made his way forward. He was mindlessly gazing out toward the horizon as his oversized boots scuffed with each step. The black tactical pants he wore were mud stained and damp. His inmate number was in bold print on the back side of his tattered jacket, down each arm, and over the left breast: C22477. The blood-stained and torn right sleeve was slowly dripping, leaving a trail behind him. A barcode was tattooed on his right wrist that matched the inmate number on his jacket. His face had a few days' worth of stubble peeking through the dried blood, dirt, and sweat stains. In his left hand he loosely held an Imperium rifle. The scuffing from his loose boots and his labored breath were the only sounds down the desolate road. The moisture from his breath rose through the chilly evening air. No wind. It was completely still, as if he had discovered an undisturbed, long-lost civilization.

In the distance two Imperium cruisers appeared on the horizon, soaring toward his direction. Joe quickly dove under an old rusty armored Imperium transporter. The visium armor would block his heat signature. He breathed anxiously, quietly, as he waited for them to pass by. Neither cruiser changed course. He had not been detected by the cruisers. "How ironic," he thought. Roughly forty-eight hours before, he was inside one of those transporters, heading to Imperium prison, again.

<hr>

Three days prior, he had made his way to a refugee camp in Des Moines. The camp had established itself inside a crumbled old big-box store building. The glass of the front doors and windows had been blown out. The paint on the exterior had been weathered, chipping, and faded.

He stepped through the broken glass and trash scattered across the floor, passing by small groups of huddled people who were staying warm around fire barrels throughout the open skeleton of the building. There were large visible cracks along the walls and throughout the foundation as he made his way inward.

Toward the back of the building a food line was serving. Slop was being scooped into whatever receptacles people had been able to salvage. Night was falling outside. The light from the fire barrels was the only light to be had, casting shadows on the wall, depicting silhouettes of past lives lost. Besides the low rumblings from the groups of people and crackling of the fires, it was relatively quiet.

Joe walked by a group where an elderly man was ranting. "We can't keep on like this. At least Imperium prison has showers. Maybe even better food."

Joe scoffed as he walked by. "He obviously has never been *in* the jail." He walked up to the food line and waited for his turn. He found an empty bowl on the table that looked moderately clean.

Joe jokingly asked; "What's today's specials?"

The server did not respond. Instead, he looked at him blankly and poured the slop into his bowl.

"My favorite," Joe said sarcastically. He looked around and found an old crate to turn upside-down for a seat. He took a deep breath and sighed out loud. The smell rising from the glop in his bowl was surprisingly enticing. "I can't be *that* hungry," he said to himself.

Bright lights flooded the inside of the store, coming from all open entrances. Imperium soldiers filed in and surrounded the encampment. "Fucking hell?" Joe took a long sip of slop before being screamed at to lie down and surrender. He took one more spoonful for spite and lowered himself onto the ground. Slowly all the refugees were herded like cattle into transporters. "That old man got his wish," thought Joe as he was forced into line right behind him.

The people were cuffed and shackled by visium-powered restraints. A red visium current chained them all together. Those who had never worn the visium cuffs tested their strength. Other than giving off an electrical surge, the cuffs did not budge. Joe sat down on the floor of the transporter next to the left inner wall. He pulled his knees in to make room for others and placed his arms over his knees. He watched as they all filed in. There was a look of loss and hopelessness in their faces, something he had seen all too often.

Across from him, on the other side of the transporter, was a small boy. He looked to be about seven years old. The little boy was testing the cuffs. He had grainy brown hair and blue eyes. The dirt on his face made his pale skin appear even whiter. There was a ferocity in him, something Joe had not seen or felt in a while. Their eyes met.

———————————

He was startled as he heard his mother call out, "Son! Come on! We need to go." He had been lost in thought, staring out his front door. His mother and father had been hurrying around all evening, packing what they could fit into bags and throwing them in their car. Yesterday their house was full of his friends celebrating his eighth birthday. "Hold your sister's hand," his mother ordered. His sister, who was four years younger, was watching ignorantly, oblivious to what was happening. In the background their television was on the local news station.

"Imperium Corporation announced that it has reached an agreement with the remaining world government officials, who surrendered earlier today. The treaty was just signed to unify all world governance under Imperium Corporation. Those who have not pledged their allegiance to Imperium will be considered enemies of the union and will be placed in custody. More on this story as it unfolds."

He did not fully understand the gravity of the situation. Less than two hours earlier, he was playing with his best friend, riding bikes. "What happened?" Joe wondered. "Why were they leaving in such a hurry?" His parents had been excited a few days prior. They had a breakthrough in their research of vigorium. They said it would save the world. "Why do they look so scared?" There had been times in the past when they had to report to the government or to Imperium headquarters, but they never had to leave so quickly.

"Let's go. Bring your sister." His thoughts had been interrupted, again, but this time by the call from his father. They went into the garage. His father grabbed his sister and quickly placed her in her car seat. His mom dragged him around to the passenger side, where he climbed into his booster. His father and mother hurried into the vehicle, looked at each other, and grabbed hands. They both looked back at their children, who they had just strapped into their seats.

"We are taking a little trip, okay?" his father said, hesitantly. Their eyes were bloodshot and tearful. Their skin looked clammy and sweaty. He had never seen them so nervous. His father looked back to their mother.

"Okay," his father said with a little nod. The vehicle reversed and backed out of the driveway.

He turned around and watched their house as they drove away. "If we are going on a trip, why do they look so sad and scared?"

———•———

A sudden jolt brought Joe's awareness back to the transporter. It had stopped. He had not had a flashback that intense in a long time. The little boy across from him was now asleep against his father. The back door opened, revealing two armed guards.

"All right, everyone, stand up. Females on the right, males on the left. *Move it!*" said one of the guards.

Terrified parents looked at each other as they began to separate into their respective lines, grabbing their children, holding them tight. They were marched out of the transporter in their respective lines, connecting with the other prisoners from the other transporters being unloaded. They were separated out, inside the large prison yard.

The yard was fenced in, with security towers every few hundred yards. Nothing could be seen beyond the fence line, as the spotlights were blinding and disorienting. They made everything beyond appear to be pitch black. Once the guards had separated the prisoners by age and gender, they were marched into the facility.

They were forced to empty their pockets and remove jewelry, belts, and shoes. They went through body scanners and were patted down by guards. All people had their right wrist examined for a barcode tattoo. Those who did not have a tattoo were separated into another line to receive their new marking. The rest of the prisoners were forced into lines that led them through the decontamination stations. Every captured person had to be sanitized and scanned for radiation. Joe was all too familiar with the process.

A prisoner is ordered into a twenty-five-square-foot stainless-steel room. The room is bare except for a small chute on a side wall. The prisoner's clothes are discarded to be sent to the incinerator. Once the prisoner is fully undressed and clothes discarded, a set of steel sliding doors opened into a similarly sized shower room.

Nozzles blanket the ceiling and walls, with a large drain in the center of the floor. High-powered jets cycle through hot soapy water, rinse water, then a sanitizing and radiation-neutralizing agent. A single sheet of red light slowly descends from the ceiling after each cycle to scan the body for any remaining radiation, viruses, bacteria, and other contaminants. The process is repeated until there are no traces detected. Once confirmed, the next set of sliding doors open.

Joe walked through them to receive a blast of air coming from all angles. The final small room had his gray prison jumpsuit, jacket, and slippers waiting on a small bench. They were about a half size too big and were in no way comfortable. Once he was clothed, the final set of doors opened. Two more armed guards were waiting. To his left a guard sat behind a desk.

Joe looked around at the sanitary and depressing surroundings. "No wonder the guards are so angry." The white brick walls against the dull concrete floor irritated his eyes. The metal rafters did a poor job of hiding the pipes and electrical conduit spidering the ceilings. Nothing about the surroundings provided comfort. "This is where hope comes to die," thought Joe.

Joe's tattoo was scanned by one of the guards. The guard moved the scanner up to his inner bicep. The scanner did not beep. The guard ordered him to remove his jacket and examined his skin. There were several scars from what looked like healed puncture wounds. Joe's tracking device had been removed.

The guard sighed as he pulled out an injector and shot another tracker into his bicep. Joe winced slightly from the pain. Behind the desk the other guard had his file pulled up on a computer screen. The guard typed on the computer. A few seconds later; "synchronization complete" is heard from the computer speakers. The guard standing next to Joe waved the wand across the newly implanted tracker until it beeped.

"Welcome back C22477. We hope you enjoy your stay," the guard at the desk said sarcastically. "Put him in C block." C Block was solitary confinement.

"Apparently I made quite an impression last time," Joe replied. "By the way, how's your nose?" During Joe's last escape from the prison, he had smashed that guard's face into the concrete floor.

"Shut up! Get him out of here," the guard ordered.

"Let's go," said the guard standing next to him as he sucker-punched Joe in the stomach and shoved him forward. C Block was in a different building from the processing station. It was more heavily guarded than general population. He would await transport along with the others fortunate enough to be placed there. The guard pushed him down onto a metal bench along the hallway leading to the loading dock.

There were two armed guards at the doors and two at the other end of the benches. There were guards walking up and down the corridors, shuffling prisoners who were being processed. Joe was cuffed and shackled. He sat alone for a few minutes, looking around. He eased his head back onto the cold stone wall. He closed his eyes and let out another sigh.

Regardless of how many times he had gone through this process, it never got easier. The faces changed, but the mood and feeling stayed the same. Looking into the faces of the newly imprisoned, Joe could tell which ones would give up and which ones would fight. He could tell which ones would be scouted for military service and which ones would be sent to the mines. How many thousands of lives had been ruined in this place?

CAPITULUM II
(CHAPTER 2)

Joe opened his eyes at the sound of a person being shoved down onto the adjacent bench. She looked to be in her late twenties or early thirties. She was slender and athletic, maybe five feet, eight inches tall. Her jet-black pixie cut was still wet. The fresh tattoo on her wrist was highlighted by reddened skin around the new ink. She slouched over, staring at the floor, looking pissed off. The number on her pant leg was IN72112.

"Not satisfied with the five-star accommodations?" Joe asked sarcastically.

Her eyes rose to glare at him and rolled back down to the floor. "Mind your own business," she snarled under her breath.

"Take it easy, cupcake. It won't be that bad," Joe said.

"What the fuck is that supposed to mean?"

Joe pointed to her new tattoo. He then showed her his, which had faded over time.

She huffed and said, "I can handle my own."

"Joe," he said after a brief silent pause.

"Herrera," she answered.

"Herrera. I'm assuming there is a first name?"

"Captain."

"Ah, Initium Novum. That explains a lot," snarked Joe.

"So does that," she said, pointing to his tattoo.

A slender older man in an Imperium officer uniform burst through the dock doors. By the ribbons on his military blouse, he looked to be a high-ranking officer. His eyes were cold. The sneer on his face asserted that either he was confident or extremely cocky. His name tag read Depravo. He walked right up to Herrera. "*On your feet*," he commanded.

"Make me," Herrera said, expressionless. She did not move, nor did she break her gaze at the floor.

Depravo grabbed a fist full of her hair and slammed her head against the stone wall behind her. "Get her on her feet," he yelled to the two nearest guards. Each guard raced up and lifted her under her arms. She was dazed and disoriented. She relied on the guards to keep her upright until she was able to gather herself. The officer lifted her chin to meet his eyes and then slapped her across the face as hard as he could with his free hand. "You are going to tell me *everything* I want," he said in a low, stern voice.

"Go to hell," she said through the spit and blood pooling on her lip.

He slapped her again, then with a backhand, and then a punch to her gut. She doubled over in pain, breathless. Her weight was held by the guards until she grounded her feet and stood up tall and proud. She glared into his eyes and spit in his face.

He wiped off the blood and spit with his sleeve. "So be it. I like it when they are feisty," he said while studying her face. He traced her jawline with the back of his middle finger. He leaned in closer and said softly, "I bet you are *really* feisty, aren't you?"

She slammed her forehead into the bridge of his nose, breaking it. The blow caught him off guard, and he stumbled backward. She flipped forward, releasing the hold the guards had on her arms. She spun a roundhouse kick that caught Depravo in the face. She dropped down and grabbed both guards at the groin, squeezed, yanked down on their testicles, and then shot upwards, giving uppercuts to both.

The commotion caught the attention of the other nearby guards. Joe grabbed Depravo from behind as he fell. He unholstered his pistol and cracked him on the back of the head. Depravo dropped like a bag of sand. Joe fired the weapon toward the guards running from the inner hallways.

Herrera grabbed the rifles from the ground and took up a kneeling firing position. Alongside Joe she fired at the guards racing down the hall. Joe pulled up one of the limp guards and used him as a human shield and slowly backed toward the loading dock.

"You know you're fucked," the guard said as he regained consciousness while they moved back toward the door. "You are trapped."

"Shut up!" Herrera said as they moved through the door. Herrera took the doorstops and jammed them under the back side of each door after it closed. She took one of the rifles and placed it between the handles of each door as an added measure. Off in the distance the flashing lights of several prison vehicles were slowly growing larger and brighter. "We have to move. *Now!*" she commanded.

Joe smacked the guard as hard as he could on the back of the head, rendering him unconscious. He then searched the guard's pockets for the keys to the handcuffs and shackles. After releasing himself and Herrera, he grabbed a multitool and a pocketknife from the guard. Joe handcuffed and shackled the guard behind his back and threw him in the back of the transport vehicle. "Get in," Joe said as he jumped in the driver's seat.

Following suit, Herrera jumped into the passenger seat. "Do you know what you're doing? How did you pick him up like that?" she asked.

He started the vehicle and slammed it into Drive. He stomped on the pedal, causing the rear wheels to break loose as it lunged forward. They quickly gained speed as the prison vehicles triangulated on their position.

"What the fuck are you doing? Are you crazy?" she said as the transporter raced directly toward the swarm of vehicles ahead. "What are you doing?" she insisted.

"Do you want to drive?" Joe yelled back as the distance between them, and the prison fleet quickly closed.

"*Do something. Do something!*" Herrera shouted, smacking Joe on the arm repeatedly.

"Shut up, shut up, shut up, shut up, *shut up!*"

It looked like it was going to be a head-on crash at almost sixty miles an hour. Herrera put her arms in front of her face anticipating the collision. At the last possible moment, Joe yanked the wheel hard to the left, smashing into the side of a smaller patrol car, bouncing off, and swerving between the trailing fleet vehicles.

As Joe regained speed, the fleet slammed on their brakes and turned around in pursuit. Shots erupted from the guard towers and pursuit vehicles. Joe began swerving, dodging shots, vehicles, and buildings.

"Where are you going?" Herrera said.

"There is a small area of the back fencing that is mostly unguarded," said Joe. "The prison yard backs up to a large ravine and thick forest."

"How do you know that? We aren't heading to the back of the camp," said Herrera.

"I know," said Joe. "I don't want them to follow us. We need some time to dig these out of our arms." He pointed to his bicep. "Okay, that building over there." He pointed to the right, to a storage shed. "In ten seconds, roll out the door and make your way there without being seen. Take this." He handed her a small pocketknife.

"No thanks; I have a rifle," Herrera answered.

"Not for protection, Captain, *to cut out the tracker*," he shouted, annoyed. "Okay, get ready. *Now!*"

Herrera rolled out on the back side of a large fuel tank and continued rolling until she was underneath, into the shadows. Joe swerved the transporter, shutting her door before the cruisers turned the corner. He hoped they did not realize she had left the vehicle. He saw an open bay door to the maintenance shop ahead.

He drove straight toward it. As he entered, he shot the door release on the side, which slammed the door shut behind him. The workers in the maintenance building began to flee in panic, as there were no guards to protect them. Joe slammed on the brakes and put the vehicle in park.

He went around to the rear of the transporter and opened the door. The guard was awake and had risen to his knees. Joe climbed into the back, keeping the pistol pointed at the guard.

"You are so fucking dead," the guard shouted.

Joe walked up to the guard and delivered a roundhouse kick to his head, knocking him unconscious again. He pulled the guard's boots and pants off. He took off his prison slippers and pants and put on the boots and tactical pants. "Thanks, buddy," Joe said as he slapped the guard on the head. He took out the multitool and jammed it into his bicep where the tracker was located. He dug around, wincing and holding himself back from yelling in pain. The device flipped out of his arm and landed on the floor of the transporter. He picked it up and put it in the shirt pocket of the unconscious guard. "Take care of that for me, will ya?"

He heard commotion outside of the bay door. He knew he had only a few seconds before the guards stormed the maintenance building. He identified a metal staircase leading to a catwalk near the ceiling. Above the catwalk was a fume vent big enough to shimmy up to the roof. That would be his way out. Guards swarmed the maintenance building after the bay door blew open. The blast sent shards of the door inward like pellets from a shotgun shell. Joe sprinted past as the building erupted in gunfire.

Joe made it to the staircase, skipping stairs as he raced to the catwalk. He returned fire as he made his way across the catwalk to the fume vent. He jumped up on the railing, slipped, and grabbed the manual crank to the fume vent with his free hand. Joe swung a leg up and caught the inside lip. He used his strength to shimmy up into the fume hood and through the vents, making his way out onto the roof.

He looked over toward the direction of the shed he pointed out to Herrera. He saw her slender silhouette disappear out of sight behind the shed. "Good, she made it," he thought. "I hope she got that tracker out."

He heard footsteps coming from the maintenance door to the roof. "That would've been nice to know about." He hunched down and ran to each side of the building to look over. "Surrounded." He knew that at any second that door was going to pop open. To the rear he looked down to the dumpster. A team of four guards were there, weapons drawn, two aimed on rear exit and two at the roof.

He yelled, "He's getting away" and began firing randomly off the left side of the building. One of the guards below ordered two of the others to go in that direction. They took off sprinting.

"Two is better than four," he said to himself as he jumped feet first into the dumpster.

"What the hell?" one of the guards said as Joe's landing startled them. "Go check it out," he said to the other guard, while keeping his aim at the opening. The other guard reluctantly obeyed, slinging his rifle over his shoulder and climbing the ladder on the side of the dumpster. He carelessly popped his head over the side to look in. Joe sprung upward, grabbed him around the neck, and pulled him over the top. He quickly rolled around and snapped his neck.

"Johnson! What the hell is going on in there?" the other guard yelled as he slung his weapon and began climbing the ladder.

Joe popped up over the top and fired a quick shot right into the guard's face. His body fell to the ground. Joe hurled himself over the edge and sprinted to the shed.

"Hey, over there!" he heard a guard yell as he dove behind the shed. As he rose to his feet, he felt the barrel of a rifle dig into the back of his head. "Don't move," Herrera whispered in a strong and confident tone.

"It's me," Joe whispered back.

"So much for subtlety," Herrera answered back and lowered her rifle.

"We've got to go. Help me with this," Joe said. He tried to pull up a manhole cover over a storm drain.

Herrera looked around and found a scrap piece of rebar. Together they pried up the cover and slunk down into the drain.

"Okay, it is roughly four hundred yards to the back fence. This leads to the drain that empties into the ravine." Joe pointed down into the black tube. "Watch out when you get to the end; there is about a fifteen-foot freefall from the opening."

"What are you going to do?" Herrera asked.

"Cause a distraction." Joe climbed back up the ladder and out of the manhole.

Herrera rolled her eyes and began crawling through the drainpipe. Joe took up a fighting position behind the storage shed. He began laying down suppressive fire, in hopes that he could hold them off long enough for Herrera to escape.

The guards continued closing in. He quickly covered the manhole and threw the rebar over the fence, into the darkness. He wanted to ensure Herrera's safety, so the storm drain was not an option for escape. The fence was electrified, so climbing it was not an option. He looked at the shed and shimmied up the slim windowsill to pull himself up onto the roof. The pitch of the roof was just enough to stay sheltered from the oncoming guards and not be seen from the ground. He lay still and as flat as he could, praying he was not found. The lights grew brighter and sounds of the closing guards grew louder. He slowed his breathing and remained as still as possible.

He heard movement from guards below. "Where'd they go?" one guard said. "They couldn't have lifted the manhole cover," said the other. "They couldn't have gone over the fence," said the other. "The shed is locked from the outside," said another. "Spread out! Follow the fence line! I want every inch of this yard covered! No one leaves until they are found!" yelled the commander. Slowly the guards spread off into different directions.

He waited for what felt like hours before making slight movements. He slinked toward the back of the roof to see if anyone was still around. He made his way to the peak of the roof and peered over. All the guards had left the immediate area to conduct their perimeter checks.

He slid off the back side of the roof, back on the windowsill, and onto the ground. He spent the next several minutes watching the pattern of the floodlights and the movements of the guards as they conducted their searches. He calculated a way to serpentine his way toward the back fence. In short bursts, from shadow to shadow, he made his way backward, avoiding detection.

Near the back fence there was another storm drain. It had a larger opening for runoff because of the ground grade and the need for proper drainage. This was the drain connected to the pipe Herrera was crawling through. "She should be close by now." Joe shimmied through the opening into the drain. As he reached the bottom, he heard the shuffling of Herrera coming toward him through the drain. He crawled into the drain to meet up with Herrera and make their way to the ravine opening.

"What took you so long?" Joe whispered down the drain.

"Joe?" Herrera replied.

"Follow my voice; you are almost here."

Herrera met up with Joe at the junction of the drains and continued to the exit. Joe grabbed the outside of the top of the drain and pulled himself up and out. He reached back in and grabbed Herrera's hand. He helped her up and out. They both rested a minute, straddling the top of the drain. The shadows cast from the flood of lights above made it impossible to see the bottom of the ravine or the side of the cliff.

"Do you trust me?" Joe asked.

"Do I have a choice?" Herrera responded.

"Directly below this drain is a small drainage pond, about eight feet deep. It is full of rocks and tree limbs, so you need to be careful in how you drop," Joe explained. "Aim for about three feet out from the end of the drain to hit it at the deepest spot."

"That should be easy…in complete darkness," said Herrera sarcastically.

"Keep heading south. The brush is thick, and the canopy is full. You should be hard to spot from the air or track on foot. There is a highway about a day and half's walk. There is an old, abandoned gas station where you can gain your bearings to reunite with your unit."

"What about you? We could use someone as 'resourceful' as you," said Herrera.

"Not my scene. I'm not Initium Novum material. I'm not exactly a team player."

"Where are you going?" asked Herrera.

"I have some things I need to check on. Besides, probably best if we split up."

"I owe you," said Herrera. "How did you know about all of this? How many times have you escaped?"

Joe rubbed his right bicep. "A few," he said.

"Here goes nothing," said Herrera as she dangled down below the drain. She swung her feet back and forth to drop about where Joe had suggested. She felt the icy chill of the water immediately as she fully submerged from the drop. Resurfacing she whispered, "Clear," after getting out of the way in anticipation of Joe dropping. She waited for several seconds, wondering what was taking him so long.

She heard commotion coming from the cliffside. As she pulled herself out of the pond, she felt a tap on her shoulder. After the initial shock and fear, her reflexes kicked in. She swung around to engage whoever was behind her. Her elbow connected with someone's solar plexus. The moonlight was enough to make out Joe's face as he hunched over in pain.

"What the hell? How did you…?" Herrera said, confused.

Gasping for air, Joe managed; "I know how…to quickly climb down…the ravine. Too hard…to explain… in complete darkness."

"You could've just followed me in, "said Herrera.

"Then I'd be wet too." Joe coughed.

"You'd be breathing better."

"Lesson learned," said Joe, gathering himself.

"You sure you don't want to come with me?" asked Herrera.

"No, best to stay clear of me. Go rejoin your unit. Get back to what you do, and don't get caught this time?"

"What about you?" Herrera asked.

"I've survived this long. I'll be fine."

"Typical man. Good luck, and…Thank you," said Herrera.

Joe gave her a slight nod and a smirk before he took off to the west. She headed south.

CAPITULUM III
(CHAPTER 3)

Joe peered out from under the transporter to watch the cruisers fly out of sight. He pulled the first aid kit from the transporter and treated the wound on his right bicep. He discarded his prison jacket and looked back to an unopened suitcase a few hundred yards back. He went back to retrieve it. He opened it, revealing women's clothing, bra, panties, and leggings. "Damn it!" he thought, looking around. He spotted a laundry service van up the road from the transporter. He slightly jogged up to the van and opened the back doors.

Inside he found some vigorium miner's gear that had been cleaned and never made it back. He dug around until he found pants, shirt, jacket, and boots that fit properly. He grabbed the rifle and the multitool. He grabbed a miner's bag, threw it on his shoulders, and continued down the highway.

A few more miles down the road, he came across a food supply truck. He found some dried beans and canned vegetables. It wasn't the greatest tasting, but it would give him some energy and sustenance until he could find something more. He threw a bag of beans and a few canned veggies into the miner's bag. The sun was setting so he decided to camp out in the food truck for the night and begin again in the morning.

Birds were chirping as he awoke to the morning light peering in through the windshield. He opened a can of peas and carrots for his breakfast meal. He found some cashews underneath the beans and threw a few bags into his pack and continued west. Imperium Prison is in what used to be Iowa. He was heading to Colorado Springs. That was his childhood home. He was hoping to find some answers there.

Imperium did a good job of erasing most of his long-term memories the last time he had been captured. He had been experimented on. They were using the visium in strange ways. Some of the others being experimented on were receiving injections; some were given inhalers. Joe was in a group who was given electric shock with the visium.

Most of the others who were being experimented on became unresponsive, stupefied, or dead. He could only remember blips and short flashes from his childhood. He seemed to be able to tolerate the pain and testing better that the rest.

During the last time he was detained, he had extensively studied the ceilings, corridors, hallways, and exits of the facility in which he was being held. To escape the previous time, he pretended to be unconscious after being shocked.

Two guards began releasing his restraints. He grabbed one guard's wrist with his freed hand. Yanking the guard's arm across his body, he used that guard's momentum to continue him onto his face, on the floor below. He followed onto the guard's back, lifting the guard's head, and slamming it back into the ground, breaking his nose.

He then jumped over the table and tackled the other guard in the room. He was able to get behind him and put him in a rear naked choke until he passed out. He then slammed the back of his head into the floor, for good measure.

The next image he remembered was being on the outside of the fence line, running through the wooded area and coming upon the gas station. He could not remember anything prior to his capture. He was alone, scared, and hyper alert.

As he went along his way, he had flashes, of what he could only believe to be his childhood and adolescence. He traveled from camp to camp, remaining isolated from the others. He would stay for only a few days at most. The night before this last capture, he had a dream of being in Colorado Springs as a child. He saw his house number during the flash he had in the transporter. Somehow, he was going to find that house.

Commanding General Malum Depravo was in the office of Commander Lambet, the officer in charge of the prison. General Depravo had once been the officer in charge of the prison and this was his old office. He examined his nose in an office mirror, wiping the dried blood from his face. His eye sockets and nose were already starting to bruise and swell from the break. His head pounded from the hit on the back of the head. He went to the office bathroom to wash his face. He left the bloody towel hanging from the side of the sink. He sat in Lambet's chair, at his desk, awaiting a report.

Lambet hurried into his office. "Sir, we have checked every inch of this facility. There is no sign of IN72112 or C22477. They escaped."

Depravo looked up from the desk to meet Lambet's eyes. He tapped his fingers on the desk in contemplation. He did not look the least bit distressed. "Lambet, you were the top of your class in the academy, correct?" he asked calmly.

"Yes, sir! If I can just…"

Depravo cut him off. "And you exceled through the ranks? You made Commander within four years? That is impressive."

"Sir, I—"

"Tell me Lambet, what is the protocol when capturing a Charlie class fugitive?" The tension in Depravo's face and hands tightened, even though his voice remained calm.

"We were given strict instruction to treat C22477 as a typical refugee as to not alarm him—"

"Answer the question, Commander!" shouted Depravo. He then gathered himself with a deep breath and straightened his uniform blouse.

"Sir, a Charlie class fugitive is to be separated from any persons he or she may be captured along with. They are to receive two to one, being guarded at all times when being transported or when otherwise detained outside of a double locked solitary confinement holding unit, sir."

"And did that happen, Commander?" asked Depravo as he slowly started putting on his uniform gloves.

"Sir, we were given orders—"

"Did you follow protocol, Commander?" asked Depravo again.

"No, sir," answered Lambet.

"Is it safe to say that had protocol been followed, he and IN72112 wouldn't have escaped?"

"C22477 has escaped three separate times. It's hard to say—"

"He wasn't a Charlie class felon before. Now tell me, Commander, why wasn't I immediately notified once he was found?" asked Depravo, noticeably angered.

"I wanted him processed and incarcerated, first," answered Lambet. "I thought my guards could handle him."

"You thought!" Depravo yelled angrily. He slammed his fists down onto the desk and stood up. He made his way around to meet Lambet. He took another deep breath. "Luckily for me, that is a problem I can fix."

"What?" asked Lambet.

"Your ability to think." Depravo pulled a syringe from his pocket and dragged the needle down the side of Lambet's face. He pressed hard enough for a small trail of blood to follow the tip on the needle.

"Sir, please?" said Lambet as his voice became shaky.

Depravo put his open hand on the shoulder of Lambet and leaned in closer. "If you wish." He smirked and jammed the syringe into Lambet's neck. Lambet yelped in pain as Depravo pushed the fluid into his body.

Within seconds the emotion disappeared from Lambet's face. His eyes looked straight forward, through Depravo. His arms dropped by his sides as he stood motionless. He was now a mindless, empty slate, awaiting orders.

"Commander Lambet," ordered Depravo, "after I leave this room, unholster your side arm, put the barrel to your head, and pull the trigger."

"Yes, sir," said Lambet robotically.

Depravo put the syringe back into his pocket and pulled his gloves from his hands. He placed them in another pocket, turned, and walked out of his office. A few steps down the hallway, he heard a weapon discharge behind him. "Guards, tend to the commander," he ordered without missing a step.

———————

Captain Herrera jogged through the woods until she came upon the gas station Joe spoke of. It was a small log-cabin-style building. It had two rusty, uncovered gas pumps in a gravel lot. The main entrance was at the end of a wooden wheelchair ramp and wooden stairs. The glass had been broken out and the screen on the door was ripped open. The screen door was hanging half off its hinges and blowing in the wind.

Herrera walked into the building to look for resources. She found a first aid kit to bandage her arm. By the tracks left in the dust she could tell that both humans and woodland creatures had been in there scavenging for food. There were two untouched cans of processed meat and a bag of sugar candy.

"Not the worst thing I've ever eaten," she thought. She found a gallon of unopened distilled water. She opened it and took a few long gulps to wash the aftertaste of canned meat and sugar off her tongue.

She decided to look around and see what other resources might be available. She took a backpack off the wall. There were a few cheap flashlights, lighters, some work gloves, and some nylon rope that she stuffed into the bag. She grabbed two water bottles to fill with the rest of the distilled water. They came with small carabineers so that she could clip them to her bag. She put the rest of the first aid kit into the bag as well. She looked around and saw a map of Iowa on the wall. It had a red X drawn in marker off Highway 18, near Upper Mississippi River National Wildlife and Fish Refuge. She assumed that this is where she was. She needed to get to an old Air Force base in what used to be Madison, Wisconsin.

After people took refuge underground, a series of tunnels were established for transit between military bases. That was the nearest point of entry for her to get back to her unit. It was going to take her a few days to walk there, but if she could get there, she could contact her unit. Along with the tunnels, a line of communication was built so that Imperium Novum could communicate. The ground and the vigorium cable provided enough insulation to keep it from being discovered above ground.

Even though many of these facilities were taken over by the Imperium army, there were still strongholds that had not been discovered. The tunnels that had been discovered had been cleared out and sealed off. With any luck the one at Madison had not. She was also hopeful that one of the towns along the way had a clothing store where she could change out of her prison attire.

She knew that she could not stay in any one area too long, as they were likely searching off grounds for her and Joe by now. She assumed she maybe had an hour or so head start. This being one of the only nearby buildings meant that it would likely be a place they would check. She felt that if she could get to the other side of the Mississippi River, she would have a better chance of not being recaptured.

She had been awake for nearly forty-eight hours but needed to get far enough away from Imperium Prison. She grabbed the bag and set out for the Mississippi River. As she walked, she stayed a few hundred feet off the highway to avoid being seen by any potential roaming patrols. This slowed her down a bit, but it was a safer alternative to being captured again.

She reached the river by midday the next day. The water was low and there were a few islands between the shores. She was grateful she did not have to swim or get her clothes completely wet again. She safely made it to the other side and began to search for a safe place to sleep. She was hopeful that the search had been called off by now. "I would kill for fire and clean clothes," she said to herself.

She did not want to attract attention to herself. She found a tree with a natural hole under some exposed roots. She gathered some brush to help hide the hole, after tucking up into it. The brush also helped to block out some of the light. Maybe she could catch a couple of hours of much-needed rest. She got as comfortable as she could, closed her eyes, and drifted off to sleep.

CAPITULUM IV
(CHAPTER 4)

Joe made it to Des Moines and found an old apartment complex where he could rest for a while. He found an apartment that was not in too bad of a shape. It had the only door that had not been kicked in. The door still closed and locked. There was furniture that was relatively well preserved. It was on the third floor of the closest building to the main road.

Out the window he saw an old retail store on the other side of a storage facility. After he got a few more hours of sleep, he would go over there and gather a few more changes of clothes and whatever resources he could find. He shut the door of the apartment and used the chain lock. He cracked open the window and closed the blinds. His room had clear visibility of the store and road. He had the metal stairs in front of the apartment from of the walkway. He would be able to hear anyone approaching and have time to react if necessary. It seemed to be a great vantage point.

A few hours later he awoke to the sounds of rattling outside. He quietly grabbed his weapon and slowly edged toward the window. He peered out the corner of the window. The noise was coming from around the side of the building near the dumpsters. He unlatched the chain to the door as softly as he could and gently opened the door. He kept a low profile as he edged along the side of the wall until he got to the end of the walkway. He crouched down as close to the floor as possible to peer around the corner. He saw two dumpsters. One had the lids open, the other was shut.

One of the lids began to bounce. He ducked back around the corner. After listening to the consistent popping of the lid on the top of the dumpster, he slowly peered back around. He looked down to see the lip pop up again. He aimed his rifle at the opening. As he placed his finger on the trigger, a furry nose appeared. A raccoon had apparently closed the lid on himself and could not get out. Joe scanned the area and did not hear or see anyone else. He used the stairs to walk down to the dumpster. He opened the lid. The racoon jumped out, hissed, and tried to claw at him. The racoon then jumped down and ran away.

"You're welcome," he said as the racoon disappeared behind another building. Joe walked across the storage facility to the store to see what he could salvage. The store was not in any better shape than any other dilapidated building he had been in the last several years. Most things of value had been taken. He was able to find underwear and socks in his size. There were a few bottles of concentrated camp soap, a couple of flashlights, a water bottle, and a camp towel.

"Now all I need is water," he thought. He looked around for another bag in which to stuff his new items. All that was left was a pink kitty backpack. "Whatever works."

He found a pitcher and filter that he could use to filter water as he went along his way. He was able to find a box of rice cereal and a bag of tortilla chips. On his way back he did a quick search through the storage facility to see if there was anything worth taking. Old, half-destroyed family heirlooms were about all that was left. He walked back to the apartment to grab the other bag and continue his way to Colorado Springs.

As he was about to leave the apartment, he heard a convoy of Imperium vehicles roll down the road. There were squad cars at the front and rear with a gun truck in between two transporters. They pulled into the store parking lot and stopped. From the apartment window, he could see the transporters open and squads of armed Imperium soldiers dismount.

"Great, a patrol." If they were sweeping the area, he knew it was only a matter of time before they checked the apartments for squatters. The door to his apartment was exposed and visible to the patrol in the parking lot. There were no other exits. He figured it would be within the hour that they were finished at the store and on their way to clear the storage units and apartment complex. What was once a vantage point was now a trap. There were enough squads to take each floor of the building plus provide coverage around the building. He was screwed.

The gun truck, front, and rear patrol cars kept gunners scanning the area as the squads entered and encircled the store. The gunner in the gun truck was aimed right at the apartment complex, scanning the windows and doors with his high-powered weapon.

"Fuck!" Panic started settling in. Different scenarios started racing in his head. There were still several hours of daylight, so he would not be able to be covered by nightfall. His only hope was for a distraction long enough for him to slip out.

He guessed that it would take him eight seconds to sprint down stairway. He would head east behind the buildings into the wooded area next to the complex. That is a long time in the eyes of a gunner scanning his sector. How could he get ten seconds? Would it be enough of a head start to beat them on foot to the woods? That would at least give him options for hiding or losing them in a maze of trees. He scanned the room looking for some sort of distraction. The lamp? TV? Pillow? He went to the bedroom window that overlooked the parking lot. If he could get a good shot at the gunner, that may buy him enough time while the patrol reacted.

As he aimed his rifle, there appeared to be some radio traffic on the patrol's end. The soldiers rallied back around the vehicles and started making their way back into the transporters. The engines fired, and they made their way toward the exit. Once they headed north to exit the parking lot, he would make his break for it. He would run east toward the wooded area, then south. The patrol began to move out, and so did he.

He ran past the other buildings toward the woods. His foot caught the curb as he jumped over. He landed face first into the grass. He tucked into a ball, bumping and tumbling his way down the hill. He heard the rumble of the vehicles fade into the distance. Other than a few new bruises and scrapes, he was good to go.

He took off southbound, staying within the cover of the woods to avoid detection from any other patrols. He came upon an old trailer park, about half of a mile down. Across the road to the west, he saw an indoor shopping mall. As he started walking toward the trailers, another patrol came racing up from the south. "What is with the increase in patrols?" He hoped it was nothing to do with Herrera. He hoped she had made it back to her unit. Maybe they should have stayed together. Maybe he should have told her what he was doing.

All he was able to find was a box of stale crackers and more canned vegetables as he searched through the trailer park. He stopped and listened to ensure there were no more patrols before crossing the road toward the mall. He ran quickly up to the backside of the mall where an employee entrance had been kicked in. He entered slowly and as quietly as possible. He heard shuffling and murmurs of people talking. He was hopeful that this was another refugee camp.

"If two patrols sped right past this mall without stopping for a raid, then what did that mean?" His concern for Herrera and himself grew. "Why did they check the store and then leave?" He crept into what used to be the food court of the mall. There was a surprisingly smaller group of people than in the last place. It looked to be maybe three different families.

He decided to engage this group in conversation, instead of remaining to himself. "Hello?" he said loud enough to hear. He took them off guard as they were all huddled around a fire, cooking some food. Once they saw his miner's outfit, they lowered their guard and invited him to get warm.

One of the families appeared to be Hispanic in ethnicity. The father was stocky and short with black hair and a tangled beard. The mother was comparable in size with long, wavy hair. They had two young children, maybe five and eight. There was an older couple, maybe in their sixties. They looked to be Western European in ethnicity. The last family appeared Asian. The parents looked to be in their forties. They had five children ranging from late teens to adolescence.

"What are you cooking?" Joe asked as he grabbed an open camp chair.

The Hispanic woman replied, "Baked beans."

Joe investigated the small pot over the fire. "That's not enough for everyone here."

"It's all we have," said the woman. "We've already been around the stores; there is nothing left here."

Joe reached into his bag and grabbed a few cans of veggies and handed them over. The woman kindly smiled in gratitude. He stuck around and shared a meal with the families. They did not ask any questions, nor did he. He thanked them for the meal and continued on his way. If he were still being searched for, he would put these families in danger if he stayed too long. He walked through the mall glancing through the stores as he walked. The woman was truthful; nothing much left. He exited out of a west entrance. The sun was setting behind the control tower of an airfield on the horizon. He could make it by nightfall. He hoped he would find something of value.

He made it to the closest hangar, just as the last bit of light escaped from view. He found an old army cot to sleep on for the night. He pushed the door shut but for a small crack. He then placed an empty five-gallon can on the backside of the door, heavy enough to stop the door from blowing open, light enough to be knocked over in the event of someone coming in. That would give him enough time to react if needed. At first light he would make his way along toward Omaha. He closed his eyes and drifted off to sleep.

CAPITULUM V
(CHAPTER 5)

Herrera was woken to the sound of barking dogs. She peered through the brush to see roaming patrols with search dogs and patrol cars. She was just outside of Prairie du Chien. "Why are they still tracking me?" she thought. They normally would have stopped by now. Did they think she knew more than she did? Was it Joe?

They were still several hundred yards away. She made a break for it and headed south along the river. She tried to stay in the marshy area, hoping to help lose her scent. Around a small bend she found an old johnboat. She decided to get in it and take it downriver.

She stopped in Boscobel and came up behind an old discount store. "I hope they have my size," she said sarcastically as she entered the store. She found a black T-shirt, black stretch pants, running shoes, socks, and undergarments. She discarded her prison attire and threw it into the dumpster out back.

She decided to go ahead and stay in the building for the night. There were a few nonperishable snacks she could eat and some more bottled water. She again heard barking dogs. She saw a squad of vehicles drive by and pull into the parking lot. "So much for staying the night?"

An Imperium supply vehicle came from the east and was stopped by the patrol. As they inspected the cargo, she decided that this was her best exit strategy. Maybe she could sneak into the bed. Maybe she could somehow take out the driver. She watched intensely throughout the inspection.

After the driver was cleared by the patrol, he looked around. The driver informed the patrol that he was going to take a quick break and headed to the backside of the store to relieve himself. This was her opportunity. She quietly slipped out the back door, came up behind him, and put her rifle to his head. He froze in terror.

"Take off your clothes," she ordered quietly.

"Look, sweetheart, if you're wanting a good time, there are better ways," the driver replied.

She grabbed the back of his head and slammed it into the brick wall. She stepped to the side as he fell backward, delivering a chop to his throat as he fell to the ground. She grabbed his Imperium jacket, cap, name badge, and pants. She quickly put them on, stuffed her hair up into the cap, and pulled the brim down low.

The name tag read "Casey." She could be a Casey, she thought. She hoped the patrol did not notice the slight difference in her stature compared to his. They were roughly the same height. He was much rounder in the midsection. She quickly walked over to the truck while the guards were distracted. She made her way to the driver's seat, climbed in, and started the vehicle. She gave a wave to the patrol while keeping her brim low as she pulled out of the parking lot.

She drove east to Lone Rock, where she decided to take a small break to stop and enjoy the sunshine. She had not stopped to enjoy her surroundings since when, she could not remember. Maybe in training? She had been so focused on her mission and her unit that she had not even had a day off in at least a year. The grass and trees were fuller and greener than she had ever seen. Maybe this was a good sign? She opened the back of the truck to discover she was driving food supplies. She took more nonperishable meals and water and stuffed them into her bag. Opening a prepackaged army meal and a bottle of water, she sat down under a shady tree. The last seventy-two hours needed some processing.

She thought about everything she had been through since she was captured. How long had she been detained? She held hope that her squad had completed its mission. She was hopeful that Joe was safe. Who was he? How did he know the prison so well? How had he been able to escape before? Who had trained him? Imperium? There was something about him. "I need to focus," she thought as she tried to shake off thoughts of him. After she felt full and rested, she climbed back into the truck. "Time to reconnect with my unit."

She then hopped on Highway 14 into Madison. She followed around the south side to, then up 151. She came upon a community sports complex. She would dump the truck here. She was unsure of its original destination but figured they would be looking for it soon enough.

She did not see any form of tracking or GPS device on the vehicle. She decided to make her way to the regional airport on foot. There is an old Army National Guard armory that was an Initium Novum stronghold.

She was flying to this stronghold with her squad when they came upon a squadron of Imperium cruisers. She had been worried about the rest of her squad since being shot down. Imperium soldiers had told her they were all killed, but that could have been an attempt at manipulation. She had to believe the mission continued. The contents of the package they were tasked with escorting back was classified. They were purposefully not informed in the event of a capture; they would have plausible deniability.

She walked onto the disserted airfield. There would not be roaming guards or any other signs of life, purposefully. One of the doors would have the Initium Novum insignia, somewhere out of view. That door would have soldiers pulling guard duty on the other side. There would be a security camera that would zoom in for face recognition. The guards would issue the challenge for the day, to which she would reply.

She was unsure exactly what that day's challenge would be but knew the responses to all the challenges. Regardless of the answer she gave, she would still be taken into temporary custody to be searched and interrogated. "At least it won't be torture," she thought.

She slowly made her way around the exterior of the building. She searched every door for the emblem. Daffodils were an old symbol of new beginnings, which is where they got their name, Initium Novum. One daffodil faced westward, with its blossom faced downward. This was in reverence to those lost. The other faced east with its blossom facing upward as a promise for a brighter tomorrow. They also used their initials I.N. to mark the door. Not everyone was a talented artist. Either would be somewhere near the door, hidden, but in plain sight.

She had scanned four doorways so far, without any sign of scratching, pencil, or other marking. She brushed off dirt and scanned the ground; nothing. As she went along the backside of the building, there was a door near dumpsters. There were initials graffitied from past lovers who had used the spot to leave their mark.

"JD+RD, PT was here, BM is awesome, I love GL…" Some written in marker, some pencil, some in chalk.

In a cluster of initials was I.N. "This has to be the door." She tapped the door and looked around for a camera. Under the gutter she was able to make out a small black circle. "Bingo."

From the other side of the door a man's voice said, "Unless you have ice cream, go away!" Ice cream was the challenge word. A normal person would say "No" or might try to answer with something related to ice cream, like flavor, toppings, or type. The passwords had nothing to do with the challenge word, which made them impossible to guess and just as hard to memorize. The password for ice cream was shoe. She took a quick second to think of a reply.

"I had your ice cream, but I dropped it on my shoe."

She heard the deadbolt unlock. The door swung open to two guards aiming their rifles at her. Herrera put her hands in the air and began to kneel. "Captain Pacifica Herrera of the Fortis Caelum command."

One of the guards spoke into the radio headset.

"Okay, Captain, you know the drill. Hands behind your back. We are taking you below."

She allowed the guards to cuff her wrists and escort her inside the building.

CAPITULUM VI
(CHAPTER 6)

Commanding General Depravo decided to stay at the prison. He went to the security room and pulled up the footage of the escape. He watched IN72112 and C22477 as they worked together, then separately, to escape. He spent hours watching from several different camera recordings, watching how C22477 moved. He remembered him from the academy. He was the top in his class, but of course, he knew he would be.

He pulled up the footage from his previous escape. He then watched hours of the experimentation done on C22477. The name he had been given by his parents was Alexander Bellator. In the academy, while they were young, Imperium erased their names and gave them a number to rid them of any individuality and assist in assimilation. C22477 had been strong-willed. Of course, he would have been too if his commanding officer had executed his parents.

He could tell that the last round of experimentation had erased some of his memory, but how much? How long? Would he regain his memory? He figured he would be heading back to his childhood home, if so. He made a call to increase the roaming patrols between the prison and Colorado Springs.

"Track him down. I want him alive. I need to know what he knows. Coordinate your efforts. I want IN72112 alive. She will likely be trying to reconnect with her unit. I want to know where that stronghold is."

He reflected on both C22477 and his sister while in training. He was the officer in charge of the training facility when they came to him. He was charged with taking special care of them, given their parents' role in the development of vigorium. He needed to know if they were special in anyway. Were they ever! They were both remarkable.

He had high hopes for both. They would have been the beginning of his new elite army. Unfortunately, his sister had died in her last escape attempt. C22477 was the only member of his family left. He had to get him back. He needed to know all his capabilities.

He walked back to Lambet's office where subordinates were still cleaning up the mess. He was impressed with how well the new serum worked. That was the first test on a live person. He needed further testing to see how long the effects lasted. He was hoping for permanency.

He picked up the phone and called down to the lab. "Start trials immediately. All ages. Whatever it takes." He then called up his executive officer. "Increase patrols everywhere. We need bodies. This is no longer a prison. It's a training facility." He hung up the phone and pulled out the syringe. He stared at the remnants left inside. This solution gave control of the world to whoever controlled it.

He had been a loyal subject of Imperium and made his way to the top. Only the board members were over him. If he could perfect the solution; no one could stop him. He could be the ruler of the world. He had the best of the remaining scientists in the lab a few floors below him. He needed C22477. He needed to know what secrets his DNA possessed. He needed to know what his parents unlocked in vigorium.

Joe woke from his first full night of sleep in several days. He collected his things and scanned the inside of the building one last time before heading toward the door. The can had not been disturbed since he placed it the evening before. He slid it back and peered out of the crack of the door as he slowly opened it. "All quiet on airfield," he said out loud in his best DJ voice.

He walked out into the morning sun. Even though the air was slightly above freezing, the sun felt warm and welcoming. Across the flight line there was another hangar. Leaned against the outside was an old solar-powered dirt bike. He instinctively dropped and pulled up his rifle. In a crouched, ready position he slowly made his way over to the bike.

He scanned left and right as he moved across the flight line. No sounds, no movement. When he reached the bike, he realized that it had been there for several years. There was dirt and dust on the seat and no fresh tire marks through the dirt on the ground surrounding it. The tires were flat. Some of the metal had begun to rust. Just to make sure, he peered into the hangar; clear.

He walked back to the bike to see if it would start. He checked the battery gauge. Surprisingly it was full. This side of the building faced south, so it likely got a lot of sun. He turned the power on and put the bike into neutral. He cranked the ignition, and it started. This would cut his travel down significantly. This model had its own GPS system. The maps might be a little outdated, but it would cut out most of the guesswork.

He found an old manual tire pump in the hangar. He filled the tires and checked for leaks. "Good to go." He scanned the area outside the fence line for any movement. He hopped on and made his way to the exit. Off to the east he could see a patrol moving south. "My cue to leave." He took off to the west. He would make his way toward Omaha then southwest toward Colorado.

The drive to Omaha was delightfully uneventful, the first time in a week or more when he was not reacting to some sort of Imperium bullshit. He closed his eyes briefly, took a deep breath, and enjoyed the ride. He tried not to focus on the freezing air against his face. If the temperature was the worst of it, he could manage. Every hour or so he would stop, take a rest, warm up in the bright sun, relieve himself, and continue forward.

As he got nearer Omaha, he saw some movement up in the distance. He slowed to a stop and dismounted the bike. He kept a low profile and slowly walked the bike forward. When he was able to make out the tiny silhouette of an Imperium gun truck, he froze. If he could make out the silhouette, the people inside could see him through their binoculars or scopes.

He decided to get off the road and head straight south, then west to Lincoln. If there was already one patrol on the outskirts, there might be more within the city. "Seriously, what is up with the increased patrols? What is going on? Who or what are they looking for? Is something about to happen?"

He made it to Lincoln quickly, only to notice more patrols there as well. "Could they really be looking for me? Do they know more about me than I do?"

He decided to use the bike for its intended purpose and drive a straight line toward Colorado Springs, straight through old farmlands, across creeks, through fences, and whatever. The less accessible he was to the patrols, the better.

They were not going to keep him from his mission. He had to find the house from his flashback. He had to remember. He had to get back what they had taken from him. Maybe then he would know why they were so urgently patrolling all the major resource areas.

Taking a straight line toward Hastings slowed him down, but it was still faster than walking. The sun was starting to set. He had spent all day on the bike and avoided a couple of patrols. If he could make it to Hastings, he would break for the night. He would be able to make Colorado Springs tomorrow and take his time. He hoped it would jog his memory.

He was five miles from Hastings, according to his GPS. Up ahead there was a small grove of trees in a small depression in the farm field he was riding through. It would be a good place to rest for the night. The tree had a natural wind break with a drop into a small depression next to a small pond. He would curl up there for the night. He would need to allow the bike to charge a little in the morning. He had the camp soap; he could take a bath in the pond and change his underwear and socks. A small break was needed. He had been on high alert for days. Being out in the middle of nowhere was the best place to relax a bit before heading back into whatever he was about to face. There would likely be patrols in Colorado Springs, especially if they were expecting him to go back to the house from his memory.

He collected brush and weeds to make a softer bed and to use for warmth. He used his bag for his pillow. He looked up at the night sky. The stars shined brighter without any light pollution. He had not taken any time to stare up into the night sky in years. His thoughts started moving toward Herrera. He hoped she was okay. He hoped she reached her unit. There was something about her. He had only known her for a few hours, but he felt drawn to her. She was attractive. She was tough. She was smart. She was not a victim. She was not hopeless. She was not trying to take him for something or look to him to save her.

Any of the other women he had experienced over the last decade or so had been those who either wanted something from him or wanted him to do something for them. They were lost, destitute, and a complete product of their environment.

Some of them were attractive, some of them were tough, some of them were intelligent. None of them had all the things Herrera had. He should have stayed with her. He kicked himself for not telling her his plans. He has not trusted anyone for as long as he could remember, which was not very long, unfortunately. His last thought before slipping off to sleep was that he hoped to see her again.

Two days in a row he got a full night's sleep. When had that ever happened? He looked at the pond, then thought about the temperature. He remembered hearing something about a Polar Bear Club when he was younger, something about people wearing basically nothing, swimming in freezing water. He thought about taking a quick splash, rinse, and wash with the camp soap. "Can't be too bad, right?"

He grabbed the bottle of camp soap, stripped down, and jumped in the pond. "Holy shit! Oh, fuck! This is cold!" He quickly soaped up, rinsed off, and jumped out. "Why would anyone do this for fun?" He jumped back into his clothes and looked at the battery on the bike. Thirty percent; that should get him to Colorado Springs. He ate what was left of the food he had and then jumped back on the bike and took off.

By midday he made it to the Nebraska-Kansas border. Just north of the border was a small township, Alma. He stopped to rest and scavenge for food. There was a little café that he spotted as he walked around trying to loosen up from the long ride.

He found some stale saltine crackers that had not been opened and an unopened can of peanuts. "What I'd do for even some of that slop from the camp," he thought. He choked down what he'd found. Now to find something to drink. Salty crackers and salty nuts made for a dry mouth. He looked around for some water. He looked all around the kitchen, the freezer, and the dining area. He went back to the manager's office and looked through the drawers and cabinets. Hidden in the back part of one of the desk drawers was a small pint of whiskey. "Don't mind if I do."

He opened the bottle and smelled, just to make sure it was not full of chewing tobacco or something. Smelled like whiskey. He took a small sip. It had a sweet initial flavor of vanilla and honey and then a finish of cinnamon. The old familiar burn down the throat was nostalgic and welcomed. He took another sip and put the bottle in his coat pocket.

There was a small lake to the south of the city. He pushed the bike down there to sit by the shore and take in the warm sun. He wanted the bike to charge a little longer. Even though it absorbed sunlight while he was riding it, it expended energy faster than it replaced it.

Imperium would not waste its time in a small town like this, would it? To be safe he went to a portion of the shoreline that was not visible by road that still provided sunlight. After about another hour the bike had charged to 40 percent.

He walked up to Highway 183 South, over the bridge, and continued his off-road path, straight toward Colorado Springs. He came upon I-70 West/ Highway 24 in Kansas. He crossed over and continued onward to the Colorado border.

Something about the Highway 24 sign sparked something in his memory, but he could not remember what. The image of the road sign burned in his mind as he made his way across the open country. The GPS identified some upcoming building as Schriever Air Force Base.

The bike skidded to a stop so fast that he almost toppled over the handlebars. A flashback hit him like a ton of bricks as he tried to catch his breath. He was in the back seat of his parents' car. He smelled the pine tree air freshener hanging from the rearview mirror. He felt the heat from the sun coming through the window. He heard a radio in the background. He saw the highway sign outside the window as the car entered the highway.

He remembered the traffic lights and the on-ramp. He remembered driving into the old Air Force base that he had been in several times before. His parents worked in one of the buildings. He was anxious and scared. His parents had been secretive.

He sat for a while trying to make himself remember more. As hard as he tried, he could not get anything else to bubble up. While frustrating, he knew this was a good sign. He had hoped as he started passing other landmarks, more memories would come flooding in.

He came upon the backside of the base and followed the fence line around to the main gate entrance. A memory of coming up to the gate in the back of his parents' car surfaced. He remembered the guards stopping them, asking them where they were headed, his parents flashing their work badges, and then being waved through. He decided to go ahead and roam around the air base before heading to find the home. He was having good fortune in his recall.

CAPITULUM VII
(CHAPTER 7)

Herrera was taken down into the hidden underground base. She was placed into a locked interrogation room. The handcuffs were removed, and two guards were placed outside the door. She waited for what seemed like an eternity, before rustling and low voices were heard outside the door.

The door opened and a shadow fell before a tall silhouette. He had a deep voice and broad shoulders. She recognized him immediately.

"Hey, Chief!" she said as he stepped into the light.

He was dark complected, with a square jawline and thick neck leading to round, sculpted shoulders. Chief Saxum was bult like an upside-down triangle. He spent all his free time in the gym, and it was very apparent. Chief Saxum had taken Herrera under his wing early in the resistance. She looked to him like a father figure, and he looked to her like a daughter. After Imperium took control, they had both lost their family.

"Captain Herrera, glad you could join us," said Chief Saxum. "Why don't you bring me up to speed?"

"Well, sir, we had just crossed the eastern border of Colorado when we were taken by surprise by unknown aircraft. They were like nothing I have ever seen before. They were sleek, quick, and agile. We engaged them, and I was hit by some new type of plasma round. I was able to land my bird just outside of Fort Dodge. What happened to my squad? Did they complete the mission? Did they get the package back to Flat Top Mountain?"

"What happened after you landed, Captain?" asked Saxum.

"Two of the Imperium aircraft landed while I was climbing out. They both already had a bead on me, so I knew I was caught. They took me to Imperium Prison and began their interrogation process. They kept me in a small cell, with no light, and barely enough room to sit. Every so often they would bring me out and put me into an interrogation room. They would turn on bright lights to try to disorient me and would stay in the shadows. If I gave an answer they did not like, I would get a random punch to the face or back of the head, beaten with a rod, shocked, waterboarded…" Her voice trailed off as she began processing what she had gone through.

"Herrera?" asked Saxum, seeing that she had gotten lost in thought.

"Oh, sorry, Chief, I was…anyway, after they realized, they weren't going to get any more out of me, they decided to transport me somewhere else. They sent me through the sanitation process and gave me this." She held up her wrist where they had tattooed her inmate number. "They implanted a tracker here." She showed the wound where she had pried it out of her bicep. "I was able to get it out before I escaped."

"How did you escape?" asked Saxum.

"As I was awaiting transport, they sat me down across from this rogue 'repeat offender.' One of their commanders came bursting through the door and tried to rattle me some more. I took the opportunity to knock him on his ass. The rogue guy who called himself Joe started helping me. He provided cover fire. He had knowledge of the grounds and how to escape. He helped me open the storm drain and told me the way to go. He fended them off to let me escape. By the time I reached the back of the grounds, he was already there, waiting to help me. He told me about an old gas station that would help me get back to you. We parted ways at that point."

"Didn't you think it odd that he happened to know exactly how to escape? The lay of the land?"

"At first, I thought he might have been a plant. No, definitely not. The way that he looked at them, no, there was more there; they had hurt him. He had at least three scars from where he had dug out trackers before. There was something unique about him, though. He almost seemed superhuman. That sounds crazy, I know, but—"

"What happened after you parted ways?"

"I ran in the direction he mentioned. I found the gas station, found some rations, and oriented myself with a map on the wall. My goal was to get here. There was a surprising increase in roaming patrols. I was almost found three more times before I made it here."

"An increase in patrols? We noticed them too. And you are sure it isn't because this 'rogue guy' isn't one of them?"

"Well, maybe, now that you mention it. I thought maybe they were after him. I ended up stealing a supply truck and drove the rest of the way. I didn't tell him where I was going or what unit I commanded."

"All right, Herrera. You have had a rough few months," said Saxum.

"Months? How long have I been gone? What is the date?"

"You were shot down in August. It is November."

"*Holy shit, sir. Jesus*! They kept me longer than I thought. What about my squad? Did they complete the mission? Did you get the package?"

"Your squad is fine, and I am sure eagerly awaiting your return. The mission was completed, thanks to you. Lieutenant Certus told me you took two of them out before you bit it."

"Ready to get back in the saddle, Chief. What's our next mission?"

"Your next mission," said the chief, "is to sleep and rest. I will brief you tomorrow. For now, shower, eat, and rest. We will head back to Flat Top Mountain after I brief you at 0600 hours."

"Yes, sir!"

***

Joe was reliving the memory as he drove the dirt bike onto the base. He followed the same path he remembered his parents driving that day. He followed the road around to a hangar. Although it was empty and trashed today, he was looking at it through his seven-year-old eyes. There was a small prop plane that had the crew door open and engines running.

His parents rushed him and his sister out of the car, grabbed all their belongings, and ushered them to the stairs of the open hatch. The family rushed into the plane and took their seats. His mother buckled their seat belts and sat down next to both. Their father went into the cockpit, said something low, then came back out and joined them in his seat.

As he buckled his seat belt, he let out a sigh of relief. "We made it, honey," his father had said as the plane started taxiing to the runway. The plane engine started roaring in anticipation of takeoff at the far end of the runway. Out the window a swarm of vehicles were heading straight toward their plane. His father started yelling; "Take off, take off, now! *Now!* Hurry!"

Before the plane could build speed, the vehicles surrounded the plane. The engines slowed to a stop as they were barricaded in. There was a loud bang on the outside of the crew door.

The pilot came out from the cockpit with an anxious and woeful look. "I'm sorry," he said. He turned and opened the door. Imperium soldiers came up the folding stairs, weapons drawn. He remembered seeing the color drain from his parents' faces. They were all escorted off the plane. His parents were handcuffed and thrown into the back of separate vehicles. He and his sister were separated as well. That was the last time he saw any of them alive.

A flood of emotion came over him. He wept hysterically. He gasped for air as he fell to the ground. He grieved his family. He grieved the childhood he never had, the adulthood he never had, the life he never had. Rage filled his heart. He pounded his fists on the ground and roared from the depth of his soul; *"No!"*

Enraged, he jumped to his feet and started walking around the hangar, searching, seeking. He needed to remember more. He was unsure of what he was looking for. He hoped something would continue to jog his memory. He threw open cabinets and drawers and kicked open locked doors. He walked through the empty corridors as memories crashed over him like endless tidal waves. Pictures and short videos lost in time flashed before him like a broken film reel.

He remembered! His parents' lab was in a secret basement under the Peterson Air and Space Museum. The entrance was through the headquarters building. There was a key code that would take the elevator to a locked floor. How would he get there without power to the building and without the key?

He leaned against the wall and put his hands over his eyes. His breathing slowed as he tried to recall the underground tunnel. He was down there only once, the day they were captured. His parents had brought them to their lab and offices to get something before they boarded the plane. Another piece of the memory from that day fell into place.

They were about to board the plane when his father said something to his mother. They raced over to the control tower, around the backside. They opened an emergency exit that did not lead inside the tower, but to the corridor to their lab.

There was an emergency stairway near the lab in case of power failure. The lab was a room about fifty feet by forty feet There were four island-style workstations in the center of the room that had microscopes, beakers, burners, and other lab equipment. The rear wall had storage cabinets, double-stacked freezers and chillers, and a sink and sanitizing station. The left wall had their computer desks. On the right was a large whiteboard with marker lines and equations randomly in different colors and writing styles.

His parents raced to one of the freezers and pulled out a tray of vials. "These have to stay at minus forty degrees, or they will become unstable, and our research will be ruined," said his mother. His mother and father locked eyes, looking to each other for an answer. His father looked over at one of the center tables where an injection gun lay. "No, it's not ready," said his mother. "We haven't started human trials yet."

"What other option do we have?" asked his father. "Go destroy the files on the computer."

His mother ran to the computer and quickly pounded her fingers on the computer as windows open and closed and lines of code scrolled across the screen. His father grabbed a rubber tourniquet and the injection gun from the tabletop. He pulled four syringes and stuck each one into the top of a vial and measured out each one carefully. One by one he injected all family members with their appropriate serum.

His father threw the other vials into the sink, breaking the glass and spilling the serum down the drain. His mother grabbed the emergency fire ax from the wall and smashed the hard drive of the computer. They rushed their children out of the room. His father turned on one of the burners and turned on the rest of the gas lines in the lab. "Run!" he yelled to his family as he shut the lab door behind them.

His mother grabbed his sister, and his father grabbed him. His parents sprinted up the stairwell, out the door, and back over to the hangar. As his parents rushed between buildings, he remembered seeing a line of cars with flashing lights speeding toward the airstrip.

"What did they inject into us?" he thought. "Is this why I am the way I am? Why would they do this? What were they trying to do?" Question upon question cycled through his mind. He needed to see the lab. He needed answers. He slowly made his way to the door behind the control tower. He grabbed a flashlight from his bag and clicked it on. Placing his hand on the handle, he took a deep breath and exhaled as he pulled the door open.

CAPITULUM VII
(CHAPTER 8)

Herrera was in a dimly lit concrete room. A bright light turned on overhead. She tried to shield her eyes, but suddenly realized she was strapped to a table. She tried to move her head left and right, but it was also strapped to the table. A silhouette came up from behind her head. She started to shout, "Wait," but the person shoved a towel over her face. The table slightly inverted. Water started filling her nose and mouth. She tried to fight, but the harder she fought, the more the water filled her sinus cavities. She held her breath as long as she could. She knew if she tried to breathe, it would be nothing but water. Her whole body was tense. She let out slight grunts as she pushed herself to her limits, trying not to drown.

An alarm went off. She shot out of bed and onto the floor. She oriented herself to her surroundings. She was in the bunk room; the alarm was to wake her up. It read 4:30 a.m. She was in the stronghold. She was safe. She tried to slow her breathing and stand. Her arms and legs were so shaky that she fell back to the floor. She rolled over onto her back and sat up against the wall. The undershirt she was wearing was soaked in sweat. She slowly rocked back and forth with her forearms resting on her knees. "You're safe, you're safe, you're safe…"

After a few minutes she was able to slow her breathing and body shakes enough to stand. She grabbed a towel and made her way to the shower room. She turned the water as hot as she could stand and stood motionless as the water ran over her head and down her body. She wished the water could wash away memories like it washed the dirt from her skin. The warmth relaxed her muscles and brought her awareness back to the present moment.

She washed up quickly, dried, and put on a clean set of clothes. Initium Novum basic issue: black T-shirt, gray cargo pants, black socks, and boots. She grabbed a black long-sleeve tactical shirt and put it on over the T-shirt. She looked at herself in the mirror, took two deep breaths, and walked out into the corridor.

She went down to the dining area to grab a light breakfast. She made her way through the line grabbing some oatmeal, a banana, cottage cheese, and a cup of coffee. She sat down at an empty table and began to eat.

Chief Saxum pulled up a chair opposite Herrera. "How'd you sleep?" Saxum asked.

"Oh, you know…"

"Got it," said chief. "Finish your breakfast and meet me in the conference room."

"Roger, Chief." Herrera placed her tray in the return bin, refilled her coffee cup, and walked toward the conference room.

"Intel suggests Imperium Corporation is looking for a man who looks to be in his mid-thirties; an Alexander Bellator. His RAP sheet is on screen.

Herrera came around behind Saxum to look. "That's Joe! He is the rogue repeater that helped me escape. He told me his name was Joe. Who is this guy?"

Saxum started briefing. His mother and father were scientists working on vigorium. They had made some sort of discovery shortly before Imperium took over. They attempted to flee but were caught before they could take off. Intel suggests they were creating a new secret weapon for the resistance. Their plans were lost, and all their data went missing.

Neither of them broke their silence. After Imperium was tired of torturing them, they were executed for treason. Alexander and his sister, Katherine Marie Bellator, were taken to their training camps to be converted to soldiers. Neither child was able to be converted and both escaped multiple times. His sister died during her last escape attempt. He is the only one left that can unlock his parents' secrets.

Alex's first escape was at twelve years old. He was recaptured six months later. He was sent back to training camp. It appeared that he was assimilating. He rose to be the top of his class, however, at seventeen he escaped, again. He was recaptured at nineteen. Instead of trying to retrain him, they sent him to prison because of his training specialty. He escaped at twenty-one. Recaptured at twenty-eight. He was then placed in solitary confinement for two years. They began experimentation on him.

Saxum pulled up the security camera footage of the different experiments conducted on him and his escape. "What does he know?" Herrera thought to herself. "Why did he lie to me?"

"He had been missing until this last capture, apparently," said Saxum. "It makes sense that he knew the grounds and was able to get you out."

"I wish I had known all this before," said Herrera. "I would have made him come with me."

"You really think you would have convinced him?" asked Saxum.

"I need to know why he lied. I need to find him."

"That is your next mission," said Saxum.

———•———

Joe shined his light around the dark stairwell, slowly making his way toward the lab. He found the emergency power switch and turned it on. The lights flickered for a few seconds, then came on. The lab looked like a time capsule, relatively unchanged from the way he remembered it being left. The broken beakers were still in the sink, the busted computers were still on the desk. The whole room still had the smell of the fire. Char marks were everywhere.

He walked around the room touching countertops and cabinets, as if more answers would come through osmosis, as if he could reconnect with that day. His parents did a great job of destroying the lab. Nothing was recoverable. He knew it was time to head home.

He made his way back out and jumped on the bike. As he drove out of the base, flashes of the way back home popped into his mind. He remembered the YMCA near his home. Jet Wing Drive! Chelten Road! He remembered!

He pulled into the driveway of a humble three-bedroom house. His breath shallowed as overwhelming emotions washed over him. He stood in front of the door, frozen for what felt like an eternity. "Come on, pull yourself together," he said to himself. He let out another deep breath. "Here goes nothing." He reached out his hand and opened the door.

The inside of the house had been ransacked. Furniture had been broken and cut open. Cabinets had been smashed, drawers pulled out, and walls busted open. This was not just random vandalism, Imperium was looking for something, but what?

He walked into his parents' study. Papers were all over the floor, books pulled off the shelves, picture frames broken and scattered. He reached down and picked up one of the photos and shook off the pieces of glass. It was a family photo from when he was younger. He flipped it over and read the back.

"Eli (36), Elizabeth (33), Alex (6), and Kate (2)"

Alex! His name! Alexander Nikola Bellator! Named after Alexander Fleming and Nikola Tesla. His sister, Katherine Marie was named after Katherine Johnson and Marie Curie. His sister? His sister.... He remembered; his heart sank. She died. They were teenagers. They kept escaping the training camps. She fell off the wall during her last escape…

His parents. Executed, on live TV purposefully, to make an example of them. He was forced to watch it. He fell on the floor, sobbing. "What the fuck happened to me?" How did he forget all of this? His parents were two of the lead scientists working on vigorium. What had they injected into him and his sister? They both were superior in strength, reflexes, and mental processing. Why did his parents inject them? Was that the only way to keep it from falling into Imperium hands?? Wasn't there a better way?

As he lay on the floor, he glanced under his parents' desk. He saw his dad's journal. He grabbed it and sat up. He leaned back against the desk and opened the book. He read stories from their past, school events, family vacations, promotions, breakthroughs in their research, and other major life events. At the back of the book a few pages had been ripped out. "What was on those pages? Who ripped them out?" He decided to get up and explore the rest of the house.

The rest of the house had been tossed in similar fashion. He walked through his parents' bedroom. The bed had been tossed and ripped open. The safe in the closet was hanging open. His and his sister's birth certificates, his parents' marriage license, and passports were still in there. The savings had been taken. He walked into his sister's room. Stuffed animals had been ripped open, with stuffing scattered all over the room. The dresser, closet, and bed were all destroyed.

He walked into his room. He picked up a trophy he had earned from playing childhood soccer. It felt so long ago, and yet just yesterday. The flood of memories had been overwhelming and exhausting. He looked over and saw a kid's chemistry set scattered on the floor. He remembered the excitement in his father's face when he brought it home to him.

He remembered his dad saying, "All you need is right here in the kit, son." He rummaged through the items, a beaker, a burner, and a striker. He squeezed the handle, expecting the flint to cause a spark. It did not. He turned it over to examine the strike plate. The flint was missing. On closer examination, he found that there was a hidden compartment under the steel. He pulled out his multitool and pried the cap off. Out fell a small computer chip. "All you need is right here in this kit." His father's words echoed in his head.

He grabbed his dad's old wallet and put the chip inside. He cleared a spot on the floor, flipped over the mattress, and laid down. The last few days had been draining. He was grateful that his memories were coming back. He was glad to know his own name. He needed to know what was on that chip, the only way was to find Initium Novum, to find Herrera.

The events of his previous escape played while he dreamed. Escaping through the drain, running through the woods, reaching the gas station. He had made his way north to Minneapolis. He had gone several days without food and water. He passed out under an overpass. A collective of refugees had found him. He woke after three days. He had forgotten who he was or where he had come from. One of the refugees pointed to his tattoo and the scars on his bicep. "With that many escapes, you are certainly no average Joe." Since he could not remember his name, he started going by Joe.

Alex woke up startled by a vehicle coming down the street. He peered out the window and saw a convoy coming toward the house. He quickly gathered his things and ran downstairs, through the back door, and over the privacy fence. He stealthily made his way a few blocks over without being seen and broke into another house.

He needed more answers. Maybe whatever was on that chip could provide the missing pieces. He had never seen a chip like that one before. Once the coast was clear, he would make his way back to base. Maybe there was something there he could use to access whatever was on that chip.

———————•———————

Depravo spent hours watching a rewatching the footage of C22477. He compared his movements in training and compared them with his escapes. He had invested a lot of time in training him and trying to assimilate him. He spent even more time experimenting on him. He watched how he grew in skills and abilities. He studied his growth after each experiment. No matter the situation, C22477 appeared to improve upon his abilities. Each video showed significant growth from the last.

"What did his parents create? How much was the result of the solution they created? How much was his DNA? How much was a result of the experimentation?" He scratched down his thoughts on a piece of paper as he continued reviewing the videos. The more he knew his enemy, the better he would be able to defeat him. The solution created from visium had a great first trial. How would it effect C22477?

He watched the experiments that were done on others and compared them to him. Most of the experiments ended in death, severe disability, and brain damage. C22477 was able to survive every single experiment. In the last experiment on him, visium was energized and provided to him through shock. It seemed to have the most significant impact on him. He was able to scramble his memory temporarily. "How to make it last?" he scribbled down on the paper, circled, and underlined.

He needed to see how the testing was going downstairs. If he could make it permanent, he could literally control everyone. He closed the screen in front of him and made his way down to the lab.

Dr. Castus Inquisitio was the head of the Imperium Research and Development Team. Depravo made his way into his office. "Dr. Inquisitio, how is the research going?"

"We are collecting all kinds of data now that we are beginning human trials."

"Is the serum effective?" asked Depravo.

"That depends on your definition," Dr. Inquisitio responded.

"Save the sarcasm, Doctor. I need to know if it will work against our enemies."

"Well, that's just it, sir, it depends on who your targeted enemy is. It is seventy percent effective in males between twenty-one and thirty-five. It is sixty-two percent effective in females of the same age group. It becomes more effective the older the population gets."

"What about in teenagers and children?" asked Depravo.

"We haven't started trials on those age ranges."

"And why not?" Depravo asked as his demeanor began to change.

"Sir, we started with the population most likely to be confronted in Initium Novum, and—"

Depravo cut off an increasingly nervous doctor. "And now you have it. Start on the children and teenagers immediately."

"Sir, I—"

"Do *not* question my orders!" Depravo barked angrily.

"There is more we need to research on the targeted age group," Fired Inquisitio back.

"Like what?"

"We need a more viable medium, sir. The serum is effective only at those percentages when the serum is kept below ten degrees Celsius. It becomes more unstable as it warms. As it destabilizes, it becomes toxic. We have seen it destroy internal organs, including the brain, turning it to liquid."

"I see," said Depravo, rubbing his chin. "What are you needing?"

"Right now, we are using an egg-based medium to inject the solution, similar to old-school vaccinations. We need a medium that the body can handle that can withstand higher temperatures longer. We still need to figure out why its ineffectiveness is still so high. I would assume that you would not want a thirty to forty percent chance that it would not work on whoever it was being used on.

It is also not permanent as of right now. In all the patients, it is one hundred percent effective for the first thirty minutes. Age, weight, health, gender, all impact how long it lasts. If you are using it for training, one soldier would need to be injected multiple times a day. We simply don't have the data to know how repeated injections affect the human body."

"What about other modes of transmission? Electric shock?" asked Depravo.

"In all but one patient, electricity caused permanent brain damage and death," said Dr. Inquisitio. "That is why we stopped and went with a serum, as the human body appeared to be able to accept this transmission better. Why would we go back to something that doesn't work?"

"Is there a way to combine the use of shock and the serum?" asked Depravo.

"I am sure there is—"

"Then get started immediately," ordered Depravo. He turned and began walking toward the door. He paused and looked over his shoulder. "Doctor?" Dr. Inquisitio looked up. "Should you have any reservation about testing on the children, just remember our agreement," Depravo said in a wickedly sarcastic tone.

"Yes, sir," answered Dr. Inquisitio sheepishly.

Depravo walked back into his newly acquired office and was alarmed to find someone waiting for him. His back was turned, looking out the window behind the desk. He was a man of small stature, wide around the waist. What little hair he had was gray and looked like he had not been exposed to sunlight in decades. His tailored suit made him appear more fit than he was. Even with his back turned, he had entitlement and privilege oozing out from every pore. Upon hearing Depravo's entrance, he turned to face him.

"If I had known to expect the chairman of the board, I would have rolled out the red carpet," said Depravo in his most sarcastic tone.

"Depravo, we were sad to hear of Lambet's death," said the chairman.

"Yes, it was quite tragic. His suicide was… thoughtless, to say the least," remarked Depravo.

"The board is concerned with your recent changes to the detention center."

"I felt it was time for a change. A way to truly show Imperium's strength and power. A way to ensure victory over Initium Novum."

"Experimenting on innocents? That is inhumane. That is psychotic!"

"Have you forgotten the war we have been fighting over the last thirty years? You think imprisoning 'innocents' for the rest of their lives is humane? I am giving them an opportunity to do something with their meager, insignificant little lives. I am giving them a chance to earn their station, a chance to work toward the greater good," shouted Depravo, slamming his fists down on his desk.

"Whose greater good?" fired the chairman back. "Yours?" The chairman began to slowly circle around the desk toward Depravo. "Do not think for one second that the board is not watching you like a hawk. Do not forget your place. The board has trusted you and your decision making for many years. However, lately we have begun to question your loyalty. Do not forget to whom you owe your power."

The tension in Depravo's face softened and the redness returned to normal color. He took a deep breath and forced the best smile he could. "Chairman, why would I ever cross the entity that has given me so much? I've spent my life building this empire for you; for us." Depravo put his hand on the chairman's shoulder, gently leading him toward the door. Depravo shared a genuine smile as he thought of all the ways he could kill this man, right now. "Please do not question my motives or strategy. You gave me this position to do the things necessary to ensure Imperium's triumph. Sometimes that means getting a little…dirty. You and the rest of the board's hands are clean. Let me stay here in the trenches. You won't be disappointed with the result."

"Fine. We will allow you to continue with your plan, for now. We will be watching."

"I would not expect any less," said Depravo, trying hard not to slam the chairman's head into the door frame.

"There is no shame in hanging it up, you know," said the chairman. "The board is willing to offer you a retirement that will be quite comfortable."

"That sounds wonderful, in time. I am still in my prime," said Depravo as he gave a performer's bow.

The chairman scoffed, turned away, and walked out of the office.

Depravo had another syringe in his hand, behind his back. His face was still light and smiling. The hand was so tense that that it shattered the syringe in his hand.

Luckily, he was wearing his gloves. How he could not wait to jam a syringe in that man's neck! "All in due time," he said under his breath as he waved the chairman out. He had to wait until the serum was perfected.

"Remember our agreement." Those words swirled around Dr. Inquisitio's mind as he reviewed data at his desk. He could not concentrate. The words shot threw him like the shock he was to administer to the next round of human trials. How could he get out of this? Human trials went against everything he stood for as a researcher. His career had been devoted to making the world a better place as a result of his research, not to inflict pain in pursuit of world domination.

Depravo had requested him specifically to head his research team. He and his family had been relocated to the prison to fulfill his position. Once Depravo's intention to test on prisoners was revealed, Dr. Inquisitio tried to resign. Depravo locked up his wife and children and threatened to continue his research on them, should he try to resign. That was their "agreement." His family was allowed to live if he continued to further his research. He could not resist, escape, or even take his own life. Anything that would derail his work would cause pain and death to his wife and children. He was stuck.

He hated himself for the pain he was inflicting on innocent people. He hated that his family was being used against him, that their lives were constantly in the balance. He hated Imperium for allowing all this to happen and hated Depravo even more. He was one person he would not mind inflicting any pain upon. Even if he was successful at killing Depravo, he and his family would not escape. There was no end in sight. The only option was to finish the research, to create the weapon Depravo craved. That was the only solution at this point that would ensure his family's survival and his own. He hung his head and began to sob.

CAPITULUM IX
(CHAPTER 9)

Herrera gathered her team in the conference room. This is the first time she had seen them since her capture. She walked through the door to the sound of cheers and fist pounds on the metal conference table. She could not hold back the smile when she saw her team. "All right, all right! It is good to see all your ugly mugs too! I would not have guessed that you all could have gotten uglier, but here we are."

"Imperium did not do you any favors either, Cap," said Lieutenant Certus.

Lieutenant Certus was the second in command of the team. He was like the younger brother Herrera never wanted. They had gone through the academy together. A near-death experience during training brought them together like siblings. He was loyal and honest; a poster child for the Initium Novum.

"You good, ma'am?" said Sanator. He was their medic. He was the youngest of the team. He was incredibly sharp minded and a natural empath. He had joined their team a little over a year ago, fresh out of training.

Herrera gave a slight head nod in acknowledgment.

"Of course, she is fine, Doc. Stop worrying," snarked Pares. He was the team's crew chief. He was a salty, battled-hardened warrior. He understood war on many different levels. Because of that, he was Herrera's tactical advisor. He had already served twenty-three years in Initium Novum and was soon going to be forced into retirement. After losing his family during one of the conflicts, his only sense of purpose was to see Imperium taken down for good. Herrera knew getting him to retire would be a battle all its own.

"Let's get down to business," said Herrera, regaining control of the room. "This is our target." She pulled up Alex's profile and began briefing on his background. She shared the videos of the experiments conducted on him and his multiple escapes. She shared her experience with him. "He has capabilities I have never seen in one person before. Therefore, we need to find him before Imperium. We need to know what he knows. We need to know what makes him able to withstand all the experiments, all of the torture, all of it."

"Man, that's fucked up. How could anyone survive all of that?" asked Ferox. He was the rowdiest of the bunch. He was a pure adrenaline junkie, taking severe risks in his fighting techniques that somehow always seemed to go in his favor. He was the wildest and most lucky son of a bitch Herrera had ever known.

"A person can withstand just about anything if they have a reason. Learn that reason, and you will understand," said Pares.

"Alex told me he was heading west when we parted ways. His home of record is in Colorado Springs. That is where we will begin our search. Imperium patrols have increased 60 percent over the last few weeks according to intel. It can be safe to say they are searching for him as well. They will also likely check his home of record. Be prepared for hostiles at any time during our mission. We are going covert on this one. We do not want to draw any attention to ourselves. We want to slip in an out undetected. Probus, what do you have for us?"

Probus was the tech officer. She had graduated first in her class at the academy, excelling in science and technology. She was awkward and introverted, with a quirkiness and excitability that made the dullest of person smirk. She took over the screen and pulled up her slides.

"We upgraded the defender's shields. Once activated, the defender will not be detectible on radar. The outer shell reflects the images caught by the three hundred sixty cameras on the opposite sides to make it unseeable by the naked eye. We upgraded the engine exhaust, making it one of the quietest crafts. This will help us fly below one thousand feet without being heard." Probus attempted her best rap impression. "Low and slow is how we will roll, I mean fly, well, you get it."

"Wheels up in an hour. Dismissed," Herrera ordered. She left the conference room and headed straight to Saxum to give an update before heading out.

"Watch your six out there," said Saxum. "We just got you back. Do not want to lose you, again. Get your man and get back."

"Roger, Chief."

Herrera and her team finished all their preflight inspections before takeoff. "In and out. No messing around. We will land at the airfield and store the defenders in this hangar." She pulled up an arial view of the airfield and hangar. "Once secured, we will make our way on foot to this house." She scrolled the picture over to his childhood home. "If he is not there, we will look for any clues that might aid our search. Stay alert, stay alive" The team made its way into their defenders, lifted off the ground, and flew out the cargo bay.

"Okay team, radio silence once outside of base," said Herrera through the communications system. "Tower, this is Fortis Caelum. Going stealth in three, two, one." The com went silent as their crafts disappeared off radar.

"Fortis Caelum, this is tower, good copy on last transmission. Good luck. Tower out."

Herrera and her team soared through the air, silently mirroring the topography of the land. She could not help but wonder how well the new stealth systems would hold up in battle. So far, she was impressed. They were able to avoid a few roaming patrols undetected. They safely landed at Schriever Air Force Base and taxied the defenders into the hangar. After a quick security sweep, the team gathered around to review the next leg of their mission.

"This is our target." She pointed to the Bellator house. "Keep your eyes peeled as we make our way. We want to avoid any potential contact with Imperium. This is a recon mission. In and out, undetected."

"Roger, ma'am," they all said in unison.

"If we are lucky, he will be there. If not, hopefully we can find something that will help us to find him. Check your gear, we head out in five."

CAPITULUM X
(CHAPTER 10)

Alex packed up to set out for the air base. He looked out the window and could see the patrol was still at his childhood home. He found some granola bars in the cabinet that he stuffed into his bag. He made his way out the opposite side of the house. He was pissed that he was unable to grab the bike when he left. The patrol knew he was there, no doubt. Probably why there were there for so long. He stealthily made his way over a few more fences and across other yards. He crossed the highway and saw what looked like silhouettes walking in the distance. "Are they conducting walking patrols as well?"

He crouched behind some bushes to wait them out. He had his rifle ready, hoping to avoid a fight. As they came closer, he noticed that one of them looked familiar. "Could it be?" he said to himself. He made his way out from behind the bushes. He slung the rifle to his back and held his palms facing out and arms low. He rose his arms out an up to show he meant no harm, hoping she would recognize him before one of them fired.

"Joe?" Herrera yelled out.

"Alex, actually," he replied as they drew closer.

"So, I've learned. What the fuck?"

"Imperium fried my memory. I had no idea who I was or where I came from. Short blips of memories would come to mind randomly over the years but have increased significantly over the last few weeks. It wasn't until yesterday, in my old house that I remembered my real name."

"That's fucked up," said Ferox.

"Tell me about it. I feel like I have had the world's worst hangover, without any of the fun," said Alex.

"We saw the footage. You are one tough son of a bitch," replied Ferox.

"Let us continue this conversation later. Right now, we need to get back to base and debrief," said Herrera.

"First I need to check out my parents' lab," said Alex. "My father left me this data chip, but I have never seen anything like it. I need to see if there is something I can use to figure out what is on here." He pulled out the chip for the team to view.

"Probus, have you seen anything like this?" asked Herrera.

Probus examined the chip. "Never. It looks like it is half of an old memory drive. Look at this side right here. If there was a similar-sized piece, it would fit into the old x drive on the old computer systems."

"Half." Alex thought a moment. "We need to go back to the house. I found this chip in my old chemistry set. I bet the other piece is in my sister's room somewhere."

"Let's make it quick," said Herrera.

"Wait, there is still a patrol there. I had to leave quickly when they rolled up. They were still there about thirty minutes ago, and I haven't heard their convoy roll out."

"Then leave it; we can come back for it later," said Herrera.

"What if they find it, ma'am?" said Lieutenant Certus. "We can't risk it."

"We can't risk being captured, either," replied Herrera. "Pares, what do you think?"

"Ma'am, we are already here. It is riskier having to come here again to retrieve the missing piece. We need to recon. We can scout them out, maybe hear something, or tell by their behaviors, if they found anything. We stay hidden until they leave, or we engage if we need to."

"I agree with him," said Alex. "My parents wanted this information hidden. There is something valuable on it. Something that might help explain me or what they were working on or why they were killed."

"I really don't give a fuck if you agree with me or not, Bellator, I don't like you and don't want to be here. Your trip down memory lane might get us killed." Pares scowled.

"At ease, Pares. Okay, Lieutenant, you take Doc, Ferox, and Probus with you." Herrera pulled up a map of the area and plotted their route to the backside of the house. "Pares, Alex and I will go this way." She drew a line for them to come up on the front side.

"Just lovely," said Pares. "At least I can keep an eye on you," he said to Alex.

"Probus, these new coms? They are reliable?"

"And undetectable by anyone who does not have the tech," she replied.

"Let's do a quick com check," said Herrera. She put in her ear and eyepiece. Her team followed. "Check, check."

"Hear you, ma'am," replied Certus.

One by one they all gave the thumbs up on the radio check. "Alex, you don't leave my side," ordered Herrera. "Minimize radio traffic, just in case. Lieutenant, let me know when you are in position."

"Roger, ma'am. Okay team, let's head out."

"Stay alert, stay alive!" said Herrera as the two teams split.

———•———

Depravo listened to the radio chatter of the patrol at the Bellator house while reviewing training footage of Alex and his sister. He was hopeful to see something that could tell him more about their abilities and any potential weaknesses.

"Clear, clear, clear." The words rang out by the different team members. "The house is clear, no one here."

Depravo got on the radio and responded. "Tear that house upside down. Find something, anything."

"He was here, sir, recently," said the team leader over the radio. "There is a bike out front that has a full charge and there is a half drank bottle of water on the counter that has condensation."

"Call in Bravo and Charlie teams. I want a ten-mile radius around that house. Find him! If a squirrel takes a shit, I better know about it," yelled Depravo through the radio before he slammed down the receiver. He got up and walked down to the lab.

"Inquisitio, there better be good news for me."

"We have been experimenting with visium as a liquid metal. It is better able to handle temperature changes and is more stable than the injectable we had been using." Inquisitio cleared his throat. "The issue is in the transmission. So far it has been 100 percent lethal when introduced to the human body, regardless of age and gender."

"God damn it! Inquisitio, I want results," He slammed his fists down on the lab table. He picked up a syringe with the new liquid metal serum and pressed it against Inquisitio's face. "Maybe I should try it on your family."

A subordinate officer ran into the lab. "General, sir, we need you in the control room. It's urgent."

Depravo dragged the needle across Inquisitio's face, drawing a thin line of blood. He placed the syringe on the table. "Doctor, clean yourself up, won't you?" He turned and followed the officer out.

CAPITULUM XI
(CHAPTER 11)

Herrera, Pares, and Alex went through the back door of the adjacent house. They pulled the drapes and the blinds closed to set up their positions.

"Lieutenant, radio, check," Herrera said over the radio.

"Roger, setting up our position," Certus replied.

"Sit tight, report anything significant. Out." Herrera looked around and noticed Pares coming around the corner from the kitchen.

"Nothing salvageable in the kitchen."

"This was supposed to be a quick mission. We didn't pack much for rations." Pares shot another look of disgust toward Alex. Herrera got back on her radio. "Lieutenant, how are you all for rations?"

"We hit the jackpot, ma'am. Canned fruits and vegetables, beans, nuts. We stumbled on a doomsday prepper."

Herrera laughed. "All right. Don't get too comfortable over there. Glad you all can refit. Out."

Alex pulled out the food he had in his bag and tossed it on the table. They all gathered around, choosing their sustenance.

"Take up different positions. Pares, you take the front room. Alex, the master bedroom. Keep watch up the road for any additional patrols. I will take the rear bedroom."

Pares peered through a small gap in the blinds. "One patrol; two gun trucks, and two transporters. Gunner's alert, drivers on standby, lookouts at each corner. I would guess maybe half a dozen inside the house."

"Sixteen against seven; I like those odds." Ferox blurted over the coms.

"Easy, we are just scouting right now, Ferox. Hold your position."

"Damn, Pares, killing my dreams. Roger that."

An hour passed without much development. Alex looked out toward the air base. He replayed the memories of his parents' capture. "What was the breakthrough? What could they have been working on that cost them their lives?"

He spotted another patrol coming from the highway. He shouted out, "We got a problem. Another patrol is on its way."

"There's one coming from the west as well," Herrera replied. She got on her radio. "Hey, Lieutenant, we have two more patrols moving in. Look alive!"

"Roger, all clear on this side, we are on standby."

"They must have found something in the house," said Pares. "They are mounting up."

"Must be the other piece of this chip," said Alex walking down the hallway. "We need a new plan."

Herrera and Alex met back up with Pares in the living room. They watched as all except one gun truck left the Bellator house.

"They are looking for me, not all of you," said Alex.

"What's your point?" asked Pares.

"There is no need for any of you to be captured or killed today. Let me get caught, wait for them to leave, then you all can get back to you mission."

"You are our mission," snapped Pares. "We need to get you and that chip back to base. We need to know why you are so critical to Imperium."

"What other option do we have? They have steadily increased their patrols. They are keeping the house guarded. Do you really believe we can make it back without being caught?" retorted Alex.

"Fuck you!" Pares sneered.

"You are our mission, Alex. We also do not leave a man behind," Herrera sternly replied.

"This is why I am a loner. I didn't ask for any of this shit. I didn't want to lose my family. I didn't ask to be injected with whatever crap my parents made. I sure as hell didn't ask to be saved by you," yelled Alex.

"Will both of you shut the fuck up and be quiet?" growled Pares. "Whether you like it or not, you are coming with us. Shut up and help figure out a way to get us all out of here alive."

Herrera pulled up a map of the area. "We need to avoid the major roadways. There are likely more patrols in the area. We will wait until nightfall." Their plan was radioed to the other team.

"Roger, ma'am. We will step off at twenty-one thirty hours. Out," Lieutenant Certus radioed back.

The teams took shifts on watch while the others tried to get a little sleep. It was seven hours until they made their escape. Herrera, Pares, and Alex would leave thirty minutes behind Certus's team. They would meet back up at the hangar where their aircrafts were stored and fly back to Flat Top Mountain.

Alex was looking out the window at his old childhood home. The clock read 2045. It was his shift at lookout. He was young when they were taken into custody. He imagined an alternate life, a life without the war. He and his sister growing up, teenagers, causing trouble, graduating high school, getting married, having children of their own, coming back to that house to visit for holidays and birthdays. He wondered what she would have been like, how their relationship would have been. How he yearned for that alternate life.

His thoughts were interrupted by Herrera's restless sleep. She had been flopping around the couch for a while but was now making noises. She appeared to be having a flashback or nightmare of some kind. He found a blanket. He gently covered her and brushed the hair from her face.

She shot up, grabbing his wrist, rolling him onto the floor.

Alex deflected a punch. "It's me, it's me, it's Alex," he shouted.

Herrera stopped herself mid jab. She looked around and looked down at him. She was breathing heavily and looked embarrassed after realizing she had been dreaming. She punched him in the stomach as she stood up from being straddled over him. The bathroom door slammed shut after she stormed off.

Pares was still snoring in the recliner, completely unbothered by their scuffle. Alex went to the kitchen to look around. He found some old tea bags and a pot. Surprisingly, the stove still worked. He filled the pot from the sink and put it on to boil.

A few minutes later, Herrera came out of the bathroom and sat next to him at the kitchen table. "I'm sorry I flipped out," she said meekly.

"Forget about it. I should have known not to disturb you while you were having a nightmare," replied Alex.

"Yeah, well, like I said, I can handle my own."

"Obviously." Alex smirked. He got up and dusted off two coffee cups. He put a tea bag in each cup and poured the boiling water over both. He placed one in front of Herrera and one where he was sitting. "Better than nothing," he said as he sat back down.

She wrapped both hands around the mug and brought the rim up to her lips. The smell from the rising steam reminded her of her grandmother, who raised her. She took a small sip. "Tastes like shit." She took another sip. "Thank you."

"So, what is Initium Novum planning on doing with this technology?"

"Hopefully make the world a better place."

"You read that off of a greeting card?" Alex joked.

"Anything will be better once Imperium is taken down."

"What is going to stop Initium Novum from doing the same?"

"We are *nothing* like Imperium. How dare you!" Herrera snapped back.

"No offense, but once Imperium is taken down, there will need to be some form of government. Initium Novum is the only other established system. My parents were good people. I have no doubt they had the best of intentions but look what happened. They were murdered for their work. I was transformed to this thing, where I am hunted for my DNA. Imperium wants to make super soldiers. What is going to keep Initium Novum from doing the same?"

"It's not like that. And so, what if the technology is used for good? To take down an evil corporation?"

"That is just it. An army of super soldiers takes down one corporation, and then what? Another starts. Maybe not purposefully, maybe not initially, but that kind of power is infectious. I am just as curious as to what is on this chip, but I have half a mind to just break it right now."

"Don't! There may be more on there than what you think. You have no idea what your parents were making; no one does. We need to learn what they made, what the strengths are, and what weakness there are. We need to know why they felt it important enough to destroy. Why they felt injecting you was the only option. I hear you, and I can tell you Initium Novum is not like Imperium. There are good people at the top who want the power back to the people, who don't want an oppressed population. If you don't trust them, at least trust me."

"I do trust you. That is why I have agreed to help you, to stay with your team. I also want to take down Imperium. They have taken everything from me. I just need to know that I am not helping to replace one corrupt form of government with another."

"I saw what they did to you. I cannot imagine what you must feel," said Herrera.

"I assume they did something like that to you. Luckily those memories have not yet returned. I don't have to live in that reality, yet." Alex took a deep breath and let out a sigh. "I just need answers. I hope that whatever is on that chip, whatever is inside of me, is the key we need to change things for the better."

"Speaking of which…" Herrera looked at her watch. 2122hrs. "Lieutenant, status?"

"All good, ma'am. Doing a quick equipment check before we step out," Certus responded.

"Keep radio chatter to a minimum until we rally at the hangar."

"Roger, out."

"And now we wait," said Herrera to Alex as they began their own equipment check.

"What did I miss?" said Pares as he woke up from his nap.

"Nothing, really," said Alex. "Certus is about to step out."

Pares gathered all their equipment. "All right, we have two flash bangs, two rifles, Alex's rifle, two night-vision goggles, a pocketknife, and a multitool. Not exactly a full combat load."

The three grabbed their possessions to get ready to head out. "The last vehicle patrol drove past about ten minutes ago. We should be good," said Herrera. They left out the back door and started on the path back to the hangar. It had been quiet on the radio and there was no other movement outside of the wind. Without warning, the sound of weapons firing filled the air. The radio erupted.

"Taking fire! Doc's down! Sending out coordinates to your com," the lieutenant shouted over the radio.

The three took off in a dead sprint toward the other team's location. The other team had made it to the entrance of the airbase when it had encountered a roaming patrol leaving. The team was outnumbered and trying to take cover in the guard shack, or what was left of it.

"Reinforcements are likely already on the way. We need to get them out of there," Herrera yelled in between breaths as she was running.

"We need to draw their fire toward us," Pares yelled back as he raised his rifle and started shooting at the impenetrable gun truck.

"Are you fucking crazy?" yelled Alex as he raised his pistol and began shooting toward the circled patrol.

"This isn't the plan," yelled Herrera as she followed suit.

"Adapt and overcome, Captain," shouted Pares as the patrol began shifting their fire toward the three.

"Separate!" yelled Herrera. "Give them more than one target."

Herrera shifted her running toward the north. Pares shifted toward the south. Alex continued his path straight eastward, toward the guard shack. They had a brief window of opportunity to confuse the patrol and get their teammates out. Alex calculated as he ran.

"If one gun truck focused on Herrera and one on Pares, that left the transporter to him. If it was full of soldiers, they were screwed," he thought to himself as he raced toward the truck. His heart sank as he saw the rear hatch open and a squad of soldiers jump out. Time seemed to slow down as he tried to strategize and take in his surroundings.

Herrera was drawing the fire from one gun truck to the north. She was severely outgunned and slowly losing ground. The same could be said for Pares as he was facing a similar predicament. Alex was drawing fire from some of the soldiers coming out of the transporter while the others were still firing upon the guard shack. His focus intensified on the soldiers firing on him.

His mind had never been able to operate at this level, at least not that he remembered. He was able to keep his momentum while drawing a steady bead on the soldiers in front of him. In five quick, precise shots, he took out each of the soldiers firing at him. He shifted his trajectory slightly to gain a good picture of those firing on the guard shack. With another three shots, he took out the remaining soldiers. He jumped the barrier and landed right next to Certus, who was tending to Doc.

His mind was still in overdrive as he took in the scene. With the fire on them ceasing, both Certus and Probus were tending to Doc. He had wounds to his left leg and arm. They had applied a torniquet to both wounds and were giving him pain meds from his med bag.

"We have to go, *now*," yelled Alex as he picked him up into a fireman's carry. Certus and Probus were still in shock of his superhero entrance into the remnants of the shack. They grabbed their weapons and followed Alex out of the shack.

"Which hangar are your aircraft in?" Alex yelled back to Certus.

"Up on your left," yelled Certus as they were providing suppressive fire behind him as they ran.

"We are going to make it," Alex said to himself, as if he was willing it to happen. He was closing in on the hangar door as it opened in front of him. Time slowed down again as he saw a familiar silhouette emerge with a platoon of soldiers behind him.

"C22477, glad you could make it," Depravo said, mockingly as a swarm of soldiers behind him drew their weapons on the four of them. They all stopped in their tracks. Certus and Probus dropped their rifles and raised their hands. Alex flung the rifle from his hand as he kept Doc on his shoulders.

He turned back around to see both Pares and Herrera being surrounded in a similar fashion. "Fuck!"

CAPITULUM XII
(CHAPTER 12)

Depravo stormed into Inquisitio's lab. "Here is the other piece of that chip." Depravo slammed the chip down onto his table. Inquisitio had been looking at the molecular structure of his most recent serum concoction under a microscope. "Once we learn the Bellator secrets, we will have the perfect super soldier. How is the new serum working?" Depravo asked.

"The new serum is the most stable so far. We have a stable liquid metal serum that has withstood any temperature, so far. Adding a charge to it has allowed it to stabilize. With the data on this chip, we should be able to figure out how to make it survivable by the host body."

"Excellent! Start working on it immediately. Give me an update as soon as you are able to access the information on that chip." Depravo left the lab as quickly as he had entered. He was excited for the next part of his day.

Alex slowly came to, becoming aware of the sounds around him. His sight was still blurry as he blinked quickly, trying to improve his vision. He felt the weight of his body on the cuffs holding his wrists above his head. He felt the pain from the beatings to his ribs and face. He felt the sharpness of the cuts inflicted on his thighs and forearms. He felt the sweat dripping from his forehead down his arms and back.

His awareness of the last several hours came back to his mind. He heard the groanings from others and the buzzing from the lights overhead. As his vision became clearer, so did his mind. He looked around the sanitary, dull, interrogation room where he and the other teammates were hanging.

Probus was groaning. Pares was grunting, trying to find a way to break free. Herrera was coming to as well. Certus was wincing in discomfort. Ferox was still unconscious. Doc appeared to be lifeless.

Alex and Pares met eyes. Alex could tell Pares was blaming him for their current predicament. He did too. He looked over at Doc, then back at Pares, as if to ask, "Is he alive?" Pares's look gave him the answer. Doc was dead.

The locks on the steel door released, and it opened. The hinges squealed as if to foreshadow what was to happen.

"Welcome back," Depravo said sinisterly. "Are we all ready for round two? Your poor medic didn't make it through round one. Who's next?"

"Go to hell," grumbled Herrera as she slowly lifted her head.

Depravo answered with a quick fist strike to her face.

"Fuck you!" yelled Pares. He jerked on his cuffs. Blood and spit flew from his mouth.

Depravo turned his head to look at Pares. "Now, now, now, is that any way to talk to a superior officer?" He turned his head back around to look at Herrera. She wearily raised her head back up and spat blood and sweat into his face. He delivered a quick backhand before wiping his face with the other arm of his blouse. "You are fisty."

"Hey, shithead?" Alex mustered as much strength as he could. "It's me you are after."

Depravo casually made his way over to where Alex was hanging. "Yes, yes. C22477. My most prized of cadets." He slowly started walking around Alex as he spoke. "It is a shame. You and your sister were going to lead my new elite army. Too bad she had her little…accident. No matter how much pressure we put on the both of you, neither of you broke. Of all the times you two escaped, a simple slip off a wall ended it for your sister."

"Fuck off!" Alex replied.

"It made me realize that you were not invincible. That you could be stopped. That you could, in fact, be broken. That is when I started having a serum concocted that would take away that strong will of yours." The cynicism spewing from his mouth was nauseating.

The intercom in the room sprang to life. "Sir! It's a vaccine. On the chip. What he was injected with. It's a vaccine!" Inquisitio rang over the intercom. Depravo quickly ran over to it to turn it off. He pulled out his personal radio and stormed out of the room.

Before the door shut, Alex heard, "Never shout out over the intercom again." The large steel door shut, followed by the loud clank of the locks.

"A vaccine." Alex hung on those words. His parents weren't making some superhuman injection. They were making a vaccine. Something to fight off whatever Imperium was making, this serum." He looked around the room. He met the eyes of Pares, Probus, and Herrera. They had all heard it. They all had the same realization. They needed to get that computer chip. They needed to escape.

Depravo swung the door open to the lab. He walked over to Dr. Inquisitio, grabbed his lab coat with both hands, and flung him over the exam table. "The next time you get the idea to blast information over an open com, don't," he yelled at the doctor sprawled out on the floor.

"But sir, you don't understand—"

"No, you don't understand. I was interrogating them. They heard everything you said." Depravo reached down and picked him up by his lab coat. He threw his back against the table.

"The vaccine! It's the missing piece to the serum. It is exactly what we need to stabilize the serum and keep the subjects alive."

Depravo stopped, tugged at his blouse to gather his composure. He cleared his throat. "Excellent work, doctor. Start trials immediately."

"It's going to take some time to figure out dosage and—" Dr. Inquisitio was interrupted.

"You have twenty-four hours, Doctor. Call me when you have it. Oh, and Doctor? Use some discretion this time, won't you? I have an interrogation to get back to."

The next day Depravo came back into the lab. "Tell me some good news, Doctor."

"I am ready for trials. On what age group would you like me to start?"

"All of them." Depravo answered coldly.

"Sir…"

"Before you say anything, Doctor, remember our agreement."

"I know, but…"

"I've already selected a few subjects myself. I figured you wouldn't have the guts, so I chose for you. You won't even have to see their faces."

"Well actually, sir, I would. The new serum isn't injected. Just a simple drop on their forehead."

"Is that a fact? Well, then. Give me the serum, Doctor. I will do it myself."

"I must object. What if they have a violent reaction? What if I need to give emergency medical attention? What if—"

"Doctor, doctor. Don't bother with the particulars. Your reward will be what you have wanted this whole time. I will release your family. Your work is done." Depravo wrapped arm around the doctor and reached across to grab the vial. "Just a drop, right?"

"Yes, yes, sir," Dr. Inquisitio nervously replied.

"Great. Good work, Doctor."

"What, what about my family?"

"In time, Doctor. All in good time." Depravo slid the vial into his blouse pocket and left the room.

About thirty minutes later Dr. Inquisitio heard footsteps slowly walking toward his laboratory door. It was not the heavy footsteps of Depravo. It sounded like the high heels of a woman. He looked up to see his wife walk in the room.

"I cannot believe he kept his word," said Inquisitio. "Are the kids with you?"

His wife's face remained emotionless, staring blankly at him.

"Honey, what's wrong? Are you okay? The kids?"

He walked over to where she was standing and gently grabbed her arm. She stood there motionless, not even acknowledging his touch. He waved his arm in front of her face. He pinched her arm. She did not flinch. "Oh, honey, what did they do to you?"

He heard more people coming down the hall. The footsteps were light as well, and with a shorter gait. He peered out the door to see his children coming down the hall. He rushed toward them and fell to his knees. Sobbing, he reached out his arms to hug them. His children stopped just out of reach. Their faces were emotionless as well. "What is happening?" Dr. Inquisitio yelled out loud.

Depravo's voice came on over the intercom. "Congratulations, Doctor, your serum worked perfectly. I found the best test subjects. I hope you don't mind, I figured that I'd kill a few birds with one stone. I released your family as promised. I had a problem, though. I couldn't keep you all alive and free, after you made such a magnificent weapon."

Depravo began laughing as he continued. "It's a win-win, really. You got to see your family, and I got to test out your serum. Do try to enjoy your last moments with them." Depravo let out a wicked laugh.

Inquisitio ran to the counter in his lab where he had a fresh mixture of the vaccine in a beaker. He grabbed three sterile syringes and drew the vaccine into each of them. He hoped he had done the math correctly. Depravo was still laughing and speaking through the intercom. "What an arrogant piece of shit he is," he thought as he checked each one of the syringes.

Inquisitio had no idea if the vaccine would work. He had no idea how long it would take to work. He didn't even know how viable the serum was that Depravo had stolen from him. He tried not to spiral down the endless worries as he investigated the blank faces of his family. He went up to each one of them and gave them the injection.

"Kill Dr. Inquisitio," he heard Depravo say over the intercom. His wife and children began walking toward him.

"No, honey, kids, listen to me. Listen to Dad. Please! Please!" His words had no effect on his family as they closed in around him. He needed more time to see if the vaccine would work. He jumped over the table and ran to the lab door. He ran to the emergency fire hose and wrapped it around the door handle.

The door began to violently shake from his wife and children on the other side. His wife's hand burst through the glass of the door. Her newly acquired strength was enough to bend the frame with every tug. The small hands of his children started reaching through the opening. He sat down on the floor across the hallway from the lab doors, watching the hands of his sweet, loving wife and gentle children clawing through the door like wild beasts. He sat, watching, for what felt like an eternity.

The tugs started to slow. Their hands disappeared through the door, followed by thuds on the floor. He cautiously peered in through the broken glass. His wife and children had fallen unconscious on the floor. He carefully picked each of them up and laid them on gurneys. He placed restraints around their ankles and wrists. The beeps from the monitors created the most lonely and empty song Dr. Inquisitio had ever heard.

He helplessly waited at their beside. He didn't know much about the vaccine yet but was hopeful it was strong enough to reverse the effects of the evil concoction he was forced to make. His overwhelming guilt was soul-crushing as he waited for any sign that it was working. He endlessly watched their vitals, watched for movements, anything to tell him that he didn't kill the very people he was working so hard to protect.

He thought back to when he first took this position. He truly believed he was doing the right thing. He believed his research was going to end the war and bring peace. Now he was responsible for creating a serum that would quite possibly bring the end to civilization. A world of mindless drones with a mad man at the helm. "No! I must make this right. I have to stop him."

Dr. Inquisitio went to his computer and began combing through the data and the vaccine. He had to know everything about it. He had to recreate it. He had to stop Depravo. He hated himself for what he created, what he had done to his family. He drew up more vaccines from what was left and placed them in his lab coat pocket. He was going to end this.

CAPITULUM XIII
(CHAPTER 13)

Depravo was cruel enough to leave Doc Sanator's body hanging in the room. They had not been allowed to use the bathroom either. The only time they were let off the hooks holding them up was when they were being interrogated individually. The smell in that room was horrid. They were all exhausted. As far as each other knew, no one had broken.

Commotion could be heard outside of the door. It opened to the sound of the squeaking hinges. Depravo walked in with a higher-than-normal conceitedness, followed by two guards. He smugly looked around the room.

Alex had just enough energy to lift his head to look him in the eyes. "Fuck you!" Alex mustered.

Depravo slowly walked up to him. "You disgust me." He sneered at Alex. "But not to worry; that will all change soon. He smiled. "Guards, see to it that our guests get cleaned up. We want them at their best for our celebration later. They smell like shit."

One by one, the guards grabbed the team and dragged them out. They were all too weak to walk through the sanitation station, so they were each hung back up in the laundry room. Depravo's sociopathic ways continued as their clothes were cut from them in full view of the rest of the team. The fire hose reel's squeal was enough to send shivers down Depravo's spine as he strutted toward the team with the hose in hand. He looked around at the haggardness surrounding him.

"You, the feisty one," Depravo said looking at Herrera. "Ladies first." He widened his stance to brace for the watery hell he was about to unleash. Agony filled the air as Herrera's limp body waved from the water pressure like an old towel in a windstorm. Her screams pierced the sound of the rushing water, only to be muted as its drowning power blasted her face.

"Leave her alone, you sick son of a bitch," growled Alex as adrenaline surged through his body. "I swear to *God*, I am going to fucking kill you."

Depravo continued his torture undisturbed by the rants behind him. Once he was satisfied with the job he had completed on Herrera, Depravo turned to hose over to one of the guards. "Please be thorough," he ordered. "I don't want their unpleasant odor ruining the festivities."

He walked over to Herrera and lifted her chin. "Not so feisty now, are we?" He examined her soaking wet body, paying attention to every bruise and cut. Blood from her busted lip was dripping down onto her left breast. He looked back into her eyes. "It didn't have to be this way, you know?" He sneered and lowered his face down to her chest. Her nipples were hard from the cold temperature of the water and ambient temperature. The line of blood was diluted and thin as it made its way down, dripping off the tip.

Depravo stuck out his tongue and slowly licked the trail all the way up to the side of her lip. Herrera hung motionless as he awaited any response. Feeling satisfied that he had broken her spirit, he walked out of the room. One by one, each of them endured the skin-splitting pressure of water as the dirt, sweat, blood, and waste was blasted away.

They were carried into the sanitation stations to be cleaned and sanitized. They were dressed in Imperium Army uniforms and were placed in five-point restraints on metal gurneys. The guards rolled them to a service elevator that led to the roof of the building. They were lined up, side by side and stood up on end.

———————————

Dr. Inquisitio walked over to his family and kissed each one of them on the forehead. He walked over to the door lock to the cryochamber and swiped his keycard. The door opened. His status hadn't been changed. He wondered if the guards had been alerted or not. He peered out of the lab to look down the hall. There was a guard walking his way. His heart began to race as they made eye contact. The guard picked up his pace. Dr. Inquisitio frantically look around for anything he could use to defend himself.

"Dr. Inquisitio!" the guard yelled.

He was trapped. He had no experience in self-defense, no combat training. He began to raise his hands in surrender as the guard came closer. "Everything okay, Doctor? What happened to your doors?" the guard asked.

"My family has fallen ill. I'm afraid, and I need to go find General Depravo," he said as he attempted to gather himself. "I cannot leave them unattended, and the general has not responded to my alerts."

"He is going to show the board your new serum, Doctor. Do you want me to take you up there? Don't you want to be a part of the ceremony?"

"Well, like I said, I cannot leave my family unattended. Would you be willing to stay and watch over them?"

"I would need to clear it with my chain of command, so…"

"Private, trust me. I have the general's authority on this. I will clear it with your chain. Just take this communicator and inform me if there are in changes in their status."

"I don't know, Doctor, I don't want to get in trouble."

"Private, you are safe. This will all be cleared up." He handed the guard a handheld communicator and walked out of the lab. He hurried to the elevator before the guard had time to think. He had to think. He had to get the vial away from Depravo. No one else needed to suffer from that awful creation.

———————

The freezing wind burned Alex's eyes as he was stood up on end. He was grateful for the overcast, however. The natural light still felt blinding as he could not blink enough to keep his eyes from drying out. Several feet in front of them was a group of businesspeople in overpriced cold-weather gear. Depravo was between, facing the spectators.

"Distinguished board members," Depravo began. "We have entered a new era. An era that no longer has to comply with the human condition. Where soldiers can be trained without question, without mental, emotional, or spiritual barriers. An era where soldiers do what they are told the first time, every time. Soldiers who do not have to rest, who do not react to pain or exhaustion. Soldiers who can push the very envelope of human endurance.

"No longer will there be concern of loyalty among our ranks. The future is held within a single drop of this serum." Depravo pulled the vial from his coat pocket and showed it to the board members in front of him.

Dr. Iquisitio stepped out onto the roof from the elevator. A few guards gave him a nod as if he were supposed to be there. While Depravo was distracted speaking to the board members, Dr. Inquisitio walked up to one of the guards. "I need to do a quick examination of the prisoners." The guard again nodded. As he walked forward, he heard his name called by one of the board members.

"Dr. Inquisitio, while the general has given a great presentation, I would like to hear from you, regarding this serum."

Depravo spun around to meet eyes with the doctor. Trying his best to hide his surprise, Depravo continued. "Yes, Doctor, so glad you were able to join us after all. Please, share your wisdom."

"Well, it is really an amazing substance. I am sure the general has provided an overview. From what we have seen, it creates mindless drones."

The board member continued, "So you believe that this substance is the key in bringing an end to this war?"

"Sir, that solution will most definitely bring the end. What I would like to show you is the most advanced vaccine…"

"Let's not overwhelm them right now, Doctor. In fact, why don't I give the honor to you, good doctor? You should be the one to show off all your hard work."

The board members all nodded and began applauding. Depravo leaned in close to whisper into his ear.

"If you try *anything* stupid, I will personally push you off this roof myself. I don't know how you escaped or what you must have had to do to your own family, but maybe I underestimated you."

Dr. Inquisitio looked at Depravo, then turned to look at the prisoners, then the board members. He pushed Depravo back and stepped around him.

"Members of the board. We found the lost research. It's a vaccine. There are so many potentials that we haven't even begun to understand. We don't need to fight the population; we can make the world a better place. That serum makes mindless drones. That is not the way to move forward."

Dr. Inquisitio began slowly walking toward the board, pleading. "What is a world full of mindless drones? Think of all the lost innovation, lost ideas, ways to connect and grow. I beg of you, stop this from happening. Please!"

Depravo angrily walked toward the doctor. "Board members, if I may—" He was cut off.

"Dr. Inquisitio, it was you who created this serum, correct?" the head of the board asked.

"Yes, sir. And I regret it terribly."

"Why would you make it in the first place?" continued another board member.

"I had no choice. I believed I was doing the right thing. I realize now that I was wrong. I found this instead." He held up one of the syringes of the vaccine. "This was given to that man right there." He pointed at Alex. "He has endured and withstood more than I have ever seen from one person. We need to study this, study him if he is willing, to know of its potentials.

"We could end disease and famine. Imagine a world with no colds, no flu. Imagine a world with no cancer. Imagine a world united, where people were willing to come together, not through force or fear, but willingly, for the greater good."

The board members looked at each other. The head of the board stood. "We will need some time to consult on this. Depravo, what say you?"

Depravo looked as though his head would explode with rage as the veins in his neck throbbed and his face turned red. The tension in his jaw looked as though he could break steel with his teeth. "I have served this institution my entire life. I was born into this; lived it. I have devoted *everything* to our cause. I have sacrificed more than anyone. This is *my* army. This is *my* time. This vial holds the key to world domination, and its *mine!*"

Depravo quickly drew his weapon and shot each one of the board members one by one. He walked over to their bodies and robbed them of their security badges. He turned around and held them in triumph toward everyone who still had a heartbeat. He stuffed their badges in his coat pocket and walked over to Dr. Inquisitio with his weapon drawn.

"Put the serum on the prisoners, or I will shoot you where you stand," he said as he placed the gun barrel on the doctor's head.

"Whether you like it or not, you need me. There is no one who knows the inner workings of these two substances better than me. If you want to use that Black Death, you do it yourself."

Depravo hated that the doctor was right. He pressed the barrel harder into the doctor's skull. His trigger finger tensed as he looked Dr. Inquisitio in the eyes. "Fine, but you will be in front of me, just in case." He spun the doctor around and held his weapon at the doctor's back as they stepped toward the prisoners. He walked up to Lieutenant Certus.

A black tar-like substance landed on the lieutenant's forehead. His body began to seize uncontrollably as though he was being electrocuted. Red electrical charges crawled out of the substance as it spidered across his face and throughout his body. His body convulsed harder as he let out a scream of immense pain and horror.

The white in his eyes washed red. Slowly the convulsing stopped as the pain and tension faded from his face. His body fully relaxed as he became emotionless and stoic. His expression was as cold as the weather as he stood tall and hollow at attention, waiting for command.

Depravo ordered the doctor to check his vitals and unbuckle him from the gurney. Carefully the doctor slipped one of the vaccines out of his pocket. While he was unbuckling, he stuck the syringe into his thigh. He hoped it would be able to counteract the serum.

Depravo overed the lieutenant forward. Lieutenant Certus turned and walked toward Depravo. He handed the lieutenant the vial and commanded him to complete the task on the rest of his team. The lieutenant stoically grabbed the vial, turned, and walked back toward his team.

"Certus! Please! Listen to me. I know you are in there. Please! Please!" Herrera hysterically shouted.

"Please, please!" Depravo mocked as the lieutenant continued forward, unaffected by her pleas.

"You see," Depravo said in a smug, confident tone, "It is useless to resist." The narcissism exuding from his mouth was nauseating. They watched in anger as Certus, one by one placed a drop on each of their foreheads.

"You bastard! I swear to *God* I am going to fucking kill you," Herrera growled, powerless to save her squad.

Each convulsed wildly as the Black Death spread across their faces and down their bodies. The doctor secretly jabbed each one of them with the vaccine in the thigh as he unbuckled them from their gurneys. Looking into each of their blank faces was another stab in his own heart.

He had to destroy that vial. He had to destroy the research on the Black Death. In "complying" with

Depravo, he hoped he could stay alive long enough to save his family and the poor souls standing in front of him. He turned and gave Depravo a nod after he completed his task.

Depravo ordered the team to dispose of the board members and watched in satisfaction as each of them did so without hesitation. Each grabbed a body, flung it on their shoulder, and marched back into the elevator to take them to the incinerator. Depravo laughed again in evil pleasure. "The world is mine, Doctor." He shoved the vial back into his coat pocket and followed the team into the elevator. Before the doors shut, he looked at Inquisitio and said, "Get back to work. I need more of this, soon. I want an entire army by week's end.

CAPITULUM XIV
(CHAPTER 14)

Dr. Inquisitio hurried back to his lab. He was anxious for any sign of life from his family. The guard was where he was left earlier, like a good soldier.

"Thanks, Private. It is over. You may return to your station."

"How was it, Doc? Were the board members blown away?"

"In a manner of speaking, they were." remarked Inquisitio.

"I bet. I can't wait to try it."

"Slow your roll a little, Private. Don't be in a hurry to get yourself killed. Still, lots of work to be done, so please, I need my space."

With that, the private left the lab. Dr. Inquisitio pulled up all the data on the Black Death and began copying it onto a drive, then erasing it from the computer. He downloaded all the information on the vaccine and put it onto a new portable drive. He smashed the original and placed the new one in his lab coat. He grabbed all the vials and carefully placed them into a shipping container.

He wheeled each of his family members into the back of a medical transporter and secured them with their monitors all beeping in rhythm. He slid into the driver's seat and headed toward the gate. He was going to find an Initium Novum base and show them what he had done.

He pulled up to the gate where the guards ordered him to stop. He rolled down the window and showed his badge.

"Where are you heading, Doctor?" asked one of the guards.

"I have some very sick patients in the back in need of a higher level of care than I can provide here."

"You don't mind if we take a look in the back, do you, Doctor?"

"Actually, I do. They are highly contagious and unless you have hazmat gear, I suggest you let me go."

"I'm going to have to call this up. I don't see you on our list…"

"Do you see my badge? Do you know who I am? I report directly to General Depravo. This is top secret, so of course it is not on your list. Who do you think you are interfering with, on this highly classified mission? Now get out of my way before I have you all demoted."

The guards bought his rant and stepped out of the way. He hoped he could find Initium Novum before Depravo realized he was gone.

•———————•

Depravo led the team to the hangar after they dropped the bodies outside of the incinerator. His engineers had been working on a new model cruiser. Depravo had stolen the Black Death research long before he took the vial from the doctor. He gave it to his engineers so its technology could be incorporated into the design of the new cruisers.

A group of engineers were at a table toward the middle of the hangar. Beside them was a cluster of human-sized black pods in a cluster. Cables surrounding the computers on the table led from the pods to a central processor. The lead engineer looked up as Depravo and his creations walked in and met them as the continued forward.

"Are they ready?" asked Depravo.

"Not quite. They are flight ready, but we are still working on the weapons systems and armor."

"Marvelous. We have our first volunteers for their initial test flight." Depravo smirked and motioned his arm toward the team.

"Sir, I would ask for more time—"

Cutting off the engineer, Depravo said, "They are going to fly them now."

"Yes, sir." Looking toward his own team he said, "Okay, let's get them booted up."

The team of engineers began rapidly typing on their computers. Red energy surged through the cables toward the cluster of pods. A radiant red glow began to work its way from the floor to the top of the pods and seep into the crevasses and eventually pulsating from within each pod.

"All of you. Into your pods!" ordered Depravo. The outer skin of the pods began to change shape as if the pods were made from liquid mercury. They transitioned into slender cylinders just large enough for each team member to fit. The skin peeled itself back to create a doorway.

As each team stepped into their pods, Depravo walked over to the control station to watch and revel in his own glory. The technology was the most magnificent thing he had ever seen. The soldiers' vitals were on the screen. Not only were they monitoring their heartrate and oxygen saturation, but also when they needed to eat and "recharge." The components of the cruisers were also up on screen sharing similar data.

As the cruisers began to morph, the two sets of data on the screen began to merge as each person and their cruiser joined together. Depravo stood there, slowly becoming drunk in power as he looked at the monitors and the pods, thinking of all the possibilities these vehicles and his new army could provide. The excitement grew in his body until he could not handle the flood of emotion, like he was going to burst. "Launch the pods!" he yelled like hysterical Frankenstein.

———————

Alex was in hell. He was trapped in his own body. The serum had taken control of his body, but he was still in his head. He felt every sensation. He heard every command, but he had no power over his own body. He could not stop it; he could do nothing but watch in horror. He wondered if the others were experiencing the same thing or if they were fully transformed. He assumed that maybe the vaccine had somehow interacted with the serum. Either way, he was a prisoner, with a madman at the controls.

As he stepped into the pod, the liquid metal molded around him. The fluid filled his ear cavities and spread across his face. The door closed and fully incapsulated his body. The liquid visium wrapped his arms and legs. He felt pedals form under his feet and handles form into the palm of his hands at his sides. He could see inside the hangar with red outlines of the altitude, horizon, speed, energy, all as though they were projected on a screen.

He wanted to look around but did not even have control of his eyes. What he did not understand was how Depravo was able to control them, and no one else, He heard "Prepare for launch" as though someone were standing right next to him. "The technology is very impressive," he thought as he felt energy pulsating through the pod. The countdown began from the same voice in his ear as it quickly came into his mind that he did not know how to fly. "One, lift off!"

He shot upward like a cannonball until he was several hundred feet above the hangar. The pod hovered briefly while it transformed into a cruiser. His body transitioned from vertical to horizontal, as did the others, like synchronized swimmers in a pool.

Data suddenly shot into his head like an upload, and coordinates showed in front of him. He felt his fingers and feet begin to move, and just as quickly as the data, the team of aircraft shot out into the distance. His hands and feet felt every move.

He continued to try to make even the smallest movement with every bit of willpower he had. According to the coordinates, they were heading to a test site, where they could practice hitting targets and completing aerial maneuvers. He was amazed how the data flowed into and through his body to fly this ship. He had become the "brain" of one of the largest remote-controlled planes in history.

———————

Dr. Inquisitio stopped ten miles out of the prison to check on his family and disable to GPS system in the vehicle. He opened the back hatch to see his family resting peacefully as their monitors continued beeping.

He walked to the front of the vehicle and started searching for a GPS device. In not knowing what one looked like, he did not see anything out of the ordinary. He would need to find a new vehicle, and soon. He climbed back in and continued down the road.

Following the remaining road signs, he found a hospital. He was hoping to find a transport vehicle that was not one of Imperium's.

An old mail carrier van was a few blocks away from the hospital, abandoned on the side of the road. He pulled in front of it and walked around to the driver's side to see if it would start under its own power. After several failed attempts to make the vehicle start, he walked back to the rear of the medical transporter. He ripped the cables from the defibrillator and walked back around to the front of the vehicle. Carefully he wrapped the wires around the positive and negative terminals of the vehicle's battery.

"Finally!" he exclaimed out loud as the mail truck fired up. He backed it up to the rear of the medical transport and carefully transitioned his family to the back of the old van. He drove back up to the hospital to scavenge for medical supplies and extra batteries for the monitoring systems. His stomach growled as he loaded the van with needed medical equipment. He couldn't remember the last time he had eaten anything.

Inquisitio began the second leg of his journey, driving around looking for the nearest grocery store or restaurant that might have food. He stopped at a convenience store and found a few nonperishables; jerky, chips, and nuts. He grabbed the remaining bottled water and headed back out of town.

During his time working for Imperium, he bore witness to some of the torturing techniques, mainly to keep the prisoner alive through the torture. He had heard of an Initium Novum compound referred to as Flat Top Mountain. He had a general idea of where that might be. It was his only shot to save his family and anyone else from the Black Death he had created.

***

The squadron arrived at the test site where they each began testing the crafts' abilities. Alex was amazed at the agility and firepower the aircraft had. He was amazed at himself at how he was flying. The amount and size of emotions flooding through him were immeasurable. He was in awe as much as he was infuriated. He was defeated as much as he was determined not to give up.

During one of the aerial maneuvers, he felt the slightest twitch in the pinky finger of his right hand. Alex's GPS was pulled up on his display. Depravo was sending them to Flat Top Mountain. He was going to use them to attack the base. "As if he could be any more twisted," he thought. "It is a win-win for him, forcing Initium Novum to take out its own." Imperium had somehow tapped into their brains to extract the information they needed.

He was starting to get the feeling he could move both of his arms. He was afraid to test them, however. He did not know how closely his captors were watching. What would they do if he tried to take control? He wondered if the others were coming out of their forced trance. There was no way to signal them, and using the radio was out of the question. The technology in the aircraft was far more advanced than he was used to.

They had an hour before they reached their target. He decided to use the time to feel the craft around him. Imperium still had control over his gross motor functions. "Might as well learn this thing at their expense," he thought. Worse case, he would be closer to Flat Top, should he crash. "Less walking or carrying, for that matter."

Depravo made his way back to the main building. He wanted to see how Inquisitio was coming on the new serum. "Captain why aren't the bodies cleaned up yet?" he yelled into his radio.

"Yes, sir! Right away, sir!" came back through the speaker. A team of soldiers ran out from the garage door with hazmat supplies as if an oil tanker had turned over. Two by two, soldiers picked up the board members and placed them in the incinerator door. Depravo laughed watching the soldiers trying to keep the limbs of the bodies inside the door as they packed it full. It was like his own slapstick comedy show.

He got a second laugh when he saw the bent doors to the laboratory as he exited the elevator. "Dr. Inquisitio, you better have some go—" He stopped mid-sentence as he rounded the door frame into the lab. He expected some damage from the fight between Inquisitio and his family, but this was on a whole other level. Beakers were cracked, rubbish was all over the floor, cabinets and machines were broken. "Where are the bodies? Where is Inquisitio?" he thought. He walked over to the intercom. "Find Dr. Inquisitio, *now!*"

He walked over to the computer and taped on the display. A flashing cursor was all that appeared. He looked around. All the vials, all the containers, and all the applicators were gone.

The intercom interrupted. "He has fled, sir. Dr. Inquisitio is not on the grounds. He fled."

"What?" Depravo shouted and pounded his fists on the table. "Find him!" He grabbed a lab stool and flung it out the door. He raced back over to the hangars.

"Where is he? Tell me you have Inquisitio's location."

The team frantically typed on their keyboards. "Pulling up his tracker, now." The screens flashed rapidly between windows and screens. "Got him! Looks like he is heading northwest. He is surprisingly close to our flight team, sir."

"Is that so?" Depravo rubbed his chin. "I guess it is time for a dry run before they head to Flat Top. Change their target to Inquisitio. Now that we have them, we don't need him. Bring them back after they take care of Inquisitio. We will take care of Flat Top later. I want all the data; everything downloaded. Bring the final report to me as soon as possible."

Alex's brain began to spasm as he felt the changing information being forced into his head like surges of intense energy. He felt like his head was being squeezed like an orange. The whole squadron changed course, closing in on a mail truck. "What the fuck?" This target was close. What could be in that truck that was so important?

Alex's targeting system pulled up an enlarged a picture of the truck. "Dr. Inquisitio?" There was no more time for play. He was the tail aircraft of the formation. He was conflicted but knew he had to intervene. He did not want to take out the doctor or the team. After he made his move, he would not have much time before the engineers took preventive measures. Whatever he did would have to be quick and effective.

He was the right rear of their V formation. He accelerated and adjusted his ailerons to barrel role counterclockwise. He was amazed that he even knew what an aileron was. In mid-roll, he could see the top of each aircraft from his inverted position. He was impressed at the sleek body styles. They reminded him of the old B-52 bombers he read about when he was younger.

They had a "flying-wing" body like the B-52 but were much narrower. He could almost make out everyone's silhouettes within the body structure, as if they were molded to fit. The nose was about a foot in front of each head. The sides extended down toward each shoulder. Their arms extended outward and back to continue the leading edges past their feet for another half foot. Their feet were at a shoulder's width apart. The trailing edge of the wing met in between their legs at about their knees. If Batman and the B-52 had a baby, this was it. This arrowhead-looking flying machine was nothing short of a masterpiece. Too bad they had to be destroyed.

The formation was about two hundred feet above the ground, flying head-on toward the mail truck. He completed the barrel roll to end directly under Herrera's craft, who was in the lead position.

"Sir! C22477 is deviating from the flight plan. He's not responding to our commands."

"Shut him down! Override and shut him down," Depravo demanded.

The metaphorical vise was clamping tighter as he was using every bit of strength to fight the information being shoved into his brain. The power Imperium still had over his body was overwhelming. He was losing control and running out of time.

"Shut him down!" Depravo shouted as the team was panicking to gain control.

"He's fighting it, sir."

"Reroute the others to target him. Take him out!" The commands were uploaded and sent out.

Alarms were going off in the Alex's ears as the craft's defense system recognized others had locked their weapons on him. It was now or never. Alex pulled back and shot up into the belly of Herrera's craft. At the same time, he cut power to the thrusters. The force caused both his and Herrera's crafts to flip vertically. The centrifugal force caused Herrera to continue her vertical spin, to a complete inverted 180. Both craft's engines stalled, and they began to fall sideways. The remaining three aircraft crashed into them within seconds, sending all of them to earth like flaming meteors.

The aircraft crash landed within a few hundred yards from each other. They began to liquify around the teammates, pooling into dark red visium goo. An ear-piercing screech echoed in Alex's head as the remaining visium drained from his ears. He was off balance, as the visium had messed with his equilibrium, and he had a debilitating headache. The natural light from the sun burned his retinas. He fumbled several times before deciding it was best to stay on the ground until he could get his senses.

"Herrera? Certus? Pares? Ferox? Probus?" Alex yelled. Even the sound of his own voice was like an ax to his brain. The kick drum pounding of his heartbeat pulsed through his body as if his own blood was looking for an escape. He made out a blurry dark silhouette walking toward him before everything went dark.

CAPITULUM XV
(CHAPTER 15)

Alex started stirring as he heard the low, steady rhythm of an EKG in the background. He was lying on his back in a bed. He felt the soft comfort of sheets beneath him, the warmth of a blanket covering him up to his chest. He started blinking rapidly trying to clear his vision. It was dark. He saw a flickering off to the right in his peripheral vision. Dark oblong objects were off to his right. Was it all a dream? Where was he?

The weight of a dump truck fell on his chest as he slowly sat up. He was in yet another dilapidated building. The objects to the right were the rest of team, each in their own bed, hooked up to their own EKG.

"What the fuck?" Alex said under his breath as he tried to orient himself to his surroundings.

A voice came from the direction of the fire. "Welcome back," the voice said. He watched the dark figure stand and start walking in his direction. The beep on his EKG began beating faster, the closer the figure came. "Relax, Alex. It's me, Inquisitio."

"Doc?" Alex said confused. "But how? What? Where?"

"Slow down; it's okay." Inquisitio placed a hand on his arm. "After your ships crashed, I stopped to see if any of you survived. I admit I was just going to keep rolling down the road. I realized that if you all could find me, Depravo could find me."

"You had a tracker placed in your arm too," Alex said. "He had our systems lock onto your tracker. Shit! Your tracker!"

"I removed it; don't worry. I had forgotten that it was even there. I remembered when I saw the scars on your arm." Dr. Inquisitio pulled up his sleeve to show the bandaged, self-inflicted wound he had created. "I smashed it and placed it in the remains of your aircraft."

"How far away are we from the crash site?" asked Alex.

"Let me formally welcome you to Flat Top Mountain Base," exclaimed Dr. Inquisitio.

Alex looked around further. They were in what appeared to be an abandoned warehouse. The flicker from the fire was bright enough for him to make out all four corners of the building. Thick, rusty, iron beams ribbed the metal roof, with support beams interweaving between. The empty shells of the light fixtures gently swayed as if they were adrift at sea. The walls appeared to be solid concrete with a large bay door to one side and three personnel exits on each of the other walls. They were surrounded by military grade storage boxes of multiple shapes and sizes.

"Not quite the paradise Herrera made it out to be?" Alex smirked.

"We are purposefully separated from the rest of the people here. They wanted to wait until, well, either you all woke, or…" Inquisitio trailed off. He looked across the fire. The outline of beds could be seen through the flames. "My family has been unresponsive for three days now."

"What happened to them?"

"Depravo gave them the serum, just like you and the team. He had them attack me in my lab. The only hope I had was to inject each of them with the vaccine. Technically it worked. They were no longer under the control of that crazed lunatic. They blacked out, essentially. Their vitals are stable, they are breathing on their own, but they are in a coma, for lack of a better term."

Tears began to fall from Inquisitio's eyes as he turned back toward Alex. "We need to stop him. We need to stop that bastard from doing this to anyone else."

"How?" asked Alex, feeling defeated as he looked to each person motionless in their beds with the soft steady beeping from their monitors.

"You," replied Inquisitio directly. "You. You woke up. You have survived all this time. I personally witnessed the torture you were put through. I have seen how you heal, the strength you possess. You are the missing piece to this puzzle." He waved his hand across the room at each bed.

"I'm not some fucking lab rat, Doc." I am just a guy, who lost his family, who was injected with this…whatever the fuck it is. I am not your savior," snapped Alex.

"Alex, please…"

Alex ripped the IV out of his arm and the probes off his body. He swung his legs off the side of the bed and looked down at his bare legs. "Where the hell are my clothes?" He tried to stand up but lost his balance and sat back down.

Dr. Inquisitio helped him stabilize on the side of the bed. "We burned them all in fear there might be a hidden tracker in the uniforms they put you in."

"What difference does that make? They already know where this base is."

"You are right, Alex. An attack on this base is inevitable. It is just a matter of time. Please, let me run a few tests on you. Let me figure out why you are awake when the others are not. Let me figure out why you were able to regain control of your body enough to stop the attack on me. Had you not crashed, maybe you would not have lost consciousness. We need to know. Please. I beg you. Help me wake up my wife and kids and your teammates."

"They aren't my teammates. I didn't want any of this. My whole life has been forced on me. I didn't want this vaccine. None of it!"

"Alex, please." Dr. Inquisitio sat down next to the bed. "I don't pretend to know what your life has been. I know it has been tougher than most. We need to figure out how to end this war. We need to know what makes you so special. We need to know the difference between the vaccine I made and the one your parents made. You could potentially hold the key that can save the world."

Alex looked around the room again. He sat and pondered for a moment. He thought about his parents, his sister, and Herrera. "What if you're wrong? What if I don't have some magical key? What if I am just an ordinary Joe?"

"Then we go back to the drawing board. We have everything to gain. What have you to lose?"

"Okay, Doc, let's do this. But first, can I get a shower? And some clothes?"

"Of course. Let me help you walk into the facility. I will introduce you to Chief Saxum and get you feeling back to good."

"I'd settle for mediocre right about now," Alex said.

With his arm draped over Dr. Inquisitio's shoulder, he walked to the back exit. The door opened to a small space in front of an elevator. Dr. Inquisitio pushed the button, and the doors opened. The doors shut and they began their decent into the heart of the mountain.

Depravo paced around his office. A cloud of infuriation swarmed around him as he reflected on the past several days. His own cognitive dissonance blocked the realization that he was responsible for the escape of Dr. Inquisitio, his family, loss of all the data, the samples of both the vaccine and serum, and lost his elite team with the most technologically advanced fighter crafts, all within the matter of a few hours.

He needed to get the research back. The serum was his key to world domination. Now that the board was out of his way, he had complete control of Imperium and Imperium's resources. It was now time for serious damage control.

Captain Sectator entered Depravo's office. "We lost their signal, sir."

"We know where they are. That isn't the issue. Shut the door, Captain. Sit down."

The captain did as he was ordered and had a seat across from Depravo's desk.

Depravo started. "We need intel on Flat Top Mountain. We need to know its layout, defenses, everything. We need to get back what was stolen from us. We need to address the public. They need to know that the board is…dismantled. They need to know that I am now in charge. The sooner we gain public support, the easier it will be to destroy Initium Novum. We need the engineers to start building new aircraft, immediately."

"Sir, if you don't mind me asking, what happened to the board?"

"They were murdered, Captain."

"Oh, shit! By whom?"

Depravo dodged the answer. "We need to stop Dr. Inquisitio and the trial elite team. That is why an attack on Flat Top is critical."

The captain and Depravo sat for a few minutes in silence before the captain spoke up. "The mountain is a great natural barrier and defense for them. From what we know, they have fortified their base with ten-foot-thick reinforced walls that block radar and sonar from penetrating. We need someone on the inside. Someone with a tracker who could map out the installation."

The captain pulled up a visual of the outside of the mountain. Depravo reviewed the images as he thought. "Find me the most pathetic-looking young girl, "Depravo said, breaking the silence.

"Sir?"

"You said it yourself, Captain. We need inside. Who would be the easiest to gain access? An orphaned pathetic-looking little girl." The grin that appeared on Depravo's face made the captain cringe. "Blast the faces of the Inquisitio family and the trial team as fugitives. Set an award for their arrest."

"How much should the reward be?"

"Enough to entice the most hopeless hermit."

"From what source? The resources of the board members are going to be tied up for a while, addressing the next of kin and—"

"You let me worry about that, Captain. You start working on all the areas we have discussed. I want a status update by the end of the day."

"Yes, sir."

The captain stood and was dismissed.

•————————•

Inquisitio helped Alex to a shower room. "I will go grab you some clothes and a hygiene kit. I'll be back in a minute."

Alex sat down on a bench and waited. His brain was in overdrive, replaying old scenes from his childhood, from his time in training, his multiple tortures, Herrera. He pounded his fists against some empty lockers. He had not realized that he had stood and started pacing.

"Are you all right?" asked Dr. Inquisitio as he walked back in. He had general-issue cargo pants, T-shirt, underwear, socks, boots, and blouse. On top was a hygiene kit with soap, shampoo, shaving cream, razor, comb, towel, and washcloth.

"Yeah, I'm fine." He thanked Inquisitio for the supplies.

"When you are ready, Chief Saxum and I will be in the conference room down the hall to the right." The doctor excused himself from the room.

Alex turned the water on and stood under it for several minutes. The relaxing warmth helped ease the tension in his muscles as he tried to wash away to filth from the last several days. The room filled with steam before he cracked open the soap and began to bathe.

After he had completed all his hygiene, he was surprised to find that the clothing fit him well. He didn't remember telling the doctor his sizes, so he apparently was a good guesser. He laced up his boots and headed to the conference room. The chief and the doctor were discussing data that was pulled up on the screen at the back of the room. Both walked over to meet Alex.

"Mr. Bellator, it is a pleasure to meet you. I am Chief Saxum." He held out his had to shake.

"Please call me Alex. It's nice to meet you too." Alex completed the handshake and was motioned into the room.

"You sure have been through some hell. You are one tough son of a bitch," the chief said as they sat around the conference table.

Alex dismissed the comment. "So, what's the next step? What's the plan?"

"First, thank you for agreeing to help us out," the chief said. "You and the good doctor here are going to work together to figure out why you are, the way you are."

"That might take a serious amount of time," Alex said sarcastically.

"What questions do you have Alex?" Dr. Inquisitio asked.

"Well, how the hell did we end up here? Last thing I remember before passing out was a person walking toward me at the crash site."

"Like I said, I decided to stop and check on all of you to see if you survived the crash. The rest of the team was unconscious, but I saw you stumbling about, so I rushed over as quickly as I could. By the time I reached you, you had passed out as well. All of you exhibited the same traits as my family, so I knew the vaccine had begun to work. I did not have enough room in my van, so I raced to Flat Top Mountain as quickly as I could to get help. That's when I met the chief here. I told him what had happened, and he sent out a team to recover all of you."

"Why keep us out in the warehouse?"

"We didn't know what you had been exposed to," answered the chief. "For everyone's safety, especially all of yours. The good doctor was scanned for any bacteria, radiation, and diseases, as were all of you. To keep from alarming the rest of my soldiers and cause panic, we left you in the hangar until we could learn more. What other questions do you have?"

"How long was I out?"

"Thirty-six hours," Dr. Inquisitio replied.

"Fucking hell," said Alex as he wrapped his head around the situation. "The only other question I have right now is, what's for dinner?"

The chief and doctor chuckled. "I bet you are starving. Doctor, take him to the mess hall, get him some grub, then start your work."

The three men stood, shook hands, and left the room. The chief exited in the opposite direction of Dr. Inquisitio and Alex.

Alex was led to the cafeteria where he was able to gather food. The cafeteria was open twenty-four hours, so he decided to gather a bit of everything: cereal, fruit, pastry, pancakes, hamburger, fries, vegetables, soup, a slice of cake, coffee, and water.

"You sure are hungry," Dr. Iquisitio said as he sat down across from Alex.

"I haven't had real food in a long time. I am going to enjoy every bite. How are they able to produce all of this?"

"Well, mind you, I have only walked around here for a few more hours than you, but what I can tell you is they have livestock and gardens, so…" The doctor shrugged his shoulders.

"All right, so what's the game plan?"

"After you are satisfied, we will head down to the laboratory. I have met up with their research scientists, and they have begun reviewing the data on both the vaccine and Black Death."

"Black Death?"

"That is what I am calling it. Anyway, we will start simple with some labs. I want to look at your bloodwork to see what antibodies you have. I want to trace the markers for the vaccine within your system and compare it to the vaccine I created from your mother and father's research. I want to see if I missed something, or if perhaps they structured the vaccine to fit your family's DNA structure. I simply don't know what I don't know yet."

"What if there is no difference?" asked Alex.

"I also want to give you a physical exam, along with body scans to see if there was any damage caused by the Black Death. I want to see if there are any traces of it left in your body. I also want to learn of your experience while under control of the Black Death."

"That is something I want to know. How was it that Depravo was the only one who could control us?"

"So early in its development, it was 'off the books.' He didn't want anyone else know what I was working on. He told me what he wanted out of his elite soldiers, and how he wanted them to be controlled. After much trial and error, we learned that there were too many variables to create a soldier who could be controlled by certain people over others. So, with the help of his engineers, we created a remote."

"I don't understand. He was verbally giving us commands prior to being in the aircraft."

"We created a wireless router of sorts. Small enough to fit in his pocket. Eventually we graduated to one that fit in the inside of his gloves and over his pupil, like a contact. It is specific to his fingerprints and is activated by light pressure. Once activated, it syncs with the contact in his eye. A signal is sent out in the direction he is looking. The makeup of the serum interacts with the cerebral cortex, basal ganglia, and cerebellum. All these parts of your brain control your gross and fine motor functioning. It blocks signals from your own cerebrum, the part of the brain regulating thought, and accepts the signals from whoever is using the remote."

"What about while we were flying?"

"The same signal used in Depravo's remote was used in the control system of the aircraft. You basically became a 'chip' needed to fly the plane. The engineers would type in commands and send them through the craft's receiver, into your brain."

"Jesus Christ!"

"Trust me, Jesus had no part of this. Okay, so now that you have had your meal and coffee, let's go get labs. Don't pee until you get to the lab."

"Attention faithful citizens." The sound of Depravo's voice stopped both in their tracks. They turned around to view the monitor on the wall. "I have some troubling news that I must share with you." The melodramatic tone of his voice was nauseating.

"I am Commanding General Malum Depravo of the Imperium Army. I regret to inform you that our beloved board members were murdered, execution style, earlier this week. I apologize for the delay in making this public information, but it is an active investigation, and time was needed. We have identified those responsible for their deaths."

Alex, Herrera, Pares, Ferox, and Probus were plastered on the screen. "These Initium Novum murderers infiltrated the compound where the board members were meeting. This meeting was to discuss an innovation that will end this war against those ravenous rebels. If you see these criminals, please don't engage them. They are armed and highly dangerous. Call in their location promptly.

"As for the future of Imperium and our world, they were unsuccessful at thwarting our plans for a better way of life. We still have the research we need to bring about an era of peace and tranquility. I will assume the position of president for the time being, while we mourn the loss of our beloved board members and build an even stronger dynasty. Join me to help take down these would-be rebels and bring an end to this war so we can transition into the great power we were destined to be."

"Oh no!" Dr. Inquisitio said. "I thought I had erased all of that from my lab. How did he get it? He must have stolen it before I knew. Shit! This is not good."

"Okay, Doctor, let's do this. We have to figure out how to make this vaccine stronger and wipe that horrible shit out."

The two raced down the corridors to get to the lab.

Chief Saxum was waiting for them when they reached the lab. "I'm sure you saw the broadcast."

The two nodded.

"None of you are safe. They are offering 100,000 nummus per person for capture. We need to move your family and my soldiers somewhere remote."

"People don't actually believe they will pay that, do they?" asked Inquisitio.

"People are desperate. They will believe anything if it is a chance at a better life."

"What about my research, the lab? How will I continue to work?"

"We have a top-secret location where we are working on some prototypes. We have a fully furnished lab. There is only a handful of people who even know it exists. You all will be safe there. Gather all your things; we are leaving now."

CAPITULUM XVI
(CHAPTER 16)

The hangar was buzzing with life as soldiers were loading their cargo aircraft with supplies. Inquisitio's family and Herrera's team were being secured in the cargo bay. Their monitors were providing cadence to the hurried crew.

Saxum, Inquisitio, and Alex stepped off the elevator. "Begin your work as quickly as possible, Doc," Saxum said. "Alex, how are you feeling?"

"Ready to get this going, Chief. I want them all to wake up as much as you do."

Piercing light blinded the three from a patrol truck's headlights as it slid to a stop in the gravel outside the hangar door. Four silhouettes dismounted the truck. It became clear that one of them was holding something as they drew closer to the three.

"Chief!" one of them shouted.

"Lieutenant, what's your report?" Saxum asked.

"No signs of any enemy presence; route appears clear. However, we found this child out in the middle of the dessert. Poor thing must have gone days without eating." The lieutenant ushered forward the soldier holding the small child.

She looked to be about five years old. Her skin was pale and sunken in. Malnourished, she had matted brown hair and dark eyes. Her clothes were tattered and almost too small for her. Dried sand trails went down both sides of her face where it looked like she had been crying.

"Where did she come from?" asked Saxum.

"Don't know, Chief. She hasn't said a word. We picked up her heat signature while on this last patrol. We almost mistook her for a small animal. She was about ten miles out, southwest. We gave her some of our snacks and she ate them right up. She won't hardly make eye contact. She must be terrified."

"Ten miles out? There is nothing out there but desert. That is surprisingly close to where my soldiers were found. The nearest town from there is a good thirty miles or more."

"Hi, sweet girl," said the chief, softly. "My name is Cal." He motioned for the soldier to put her down. Saxum took a knee to meet her eyes. "Are you scared?"

The girl nodded.

"You are safe now. Are you hungry?"

She nodded. "Can you tell me where your parents are?"

She pointed to an Imperium crest that was on a box of rations the squad who found her had acquired along their route.

"Do you want to talk about how that happened?" asked Saxum.

The girl shook her head. Tears started falling from the corners of her eyes along the trail of dried salt and sand.

"Okay, we won't talk about it now."

The chief stood back up and addressed the lieutenant. "Take her to get some real food. Assign a female soldier to her, to help her bathe, and give her a clean set of clothes. Get her with one of our therapists to try to learn from where she came."

"Roger, Chief." The lieutenant gave the orders to his squad, and they dispersed.

The cargo craft's crew chief ran up to Saxum. "All loaded, Chief."

"Wheels up in ten."

"Roger!" The crew chief ran back to the craft.

"All right, boys, here we go." The three walked up the ramp into the hull. The pilots were going through their preflight checks as the chief walked in. "Make sure the GPS is disabled."

"Roger, Chief," one of the pilots responded.

"What does our flight path look like?"

"We will head south until we are out of range. We will circle back around and head toward our destination."

"Excellent. As soon as you finish preflight, taxi out and take off."

Chief Saxum walked back and took a seat next to Alex. He took in a deep breath and let out a sigh.

"Taking a lot of precautions to keep this place hidden," said Alex.

"Only a handful of handpicked soldiers know of its location. Anyone can be an insurgent."

"How do you know I am not?"

"I don't," said the chief. "But the situation changed. Your face was broadcasted everywhere. I can't trust my own people not to try to take you in. You also may hold the key to waking up my soldiers. The risk of you knowing where our top-secret base is a risk I must take."

The engines roared to life and the cargo carrier slowly began moving forward, out of the hangar. Within a few minutes they were ascending into the sky.

"What's the status of our package?" Depravo spoke into his intercom.

"Package has been received. Awaiting data download."

"Let me know when the download is complete."

Depravo looked out the window to the yard below. He envisioned thousands of super soldiers in formation awaiting the command to deploy. With the serum, he would no longer have to separate the healthy from the unhealthy. It would not matter. They would all be expendable. He chuckled to himself as he thought of how Initium Novum would react having to battle against senior citizens and children. The mental anguish alone would be enough to ensure his victory. He had to get that data back. They could not make a new batch without it.

The girl they selected could not have looked more pathetic. She and her mother were detained a few weeks earlier. Her father was killed in front of her while trying to protect the family from Imperium. She had not spoken since then. Her mother's life was threatened should she try to tell the truth to Initium Novum. They had placed several trackers on her clothing and injected two false trackers in her biceps. The actual tracker was inserted at the base of her skull. When she found the lab, she was to tap twice over the injection site. This would "mark" that area of the compound as she walked around.

Once that mark was placed, he would activate the insurgents. The goal was to be in and out before Initium Novum had a chance to respond. Once they had what they need, they would send in the bombers to level the mountain. The irony of the girl unknowingly being on a suicide mission to protect her mother's life amused Depravo.

The night sky from outside contrasted against the lights of his office, creating a demonic reflection of his face in the window before him. He chuckled as he turned to head back to the hangar.

———————•———————

The girl was taken to the cafeteria to eat. A young female private was assigned to her. Once she had eaten, helped to bathe, and seen by a pediatric doctor, she would be taken to the behavioral health wing of the compound to meet with a counselor. She would be assigned to the orphan bay where she could integrate with the other orphaned children. The chief placed an urgency on trying to get her to speak. He rightly had concerns with how she ended up in the middle of nowhere. He suspected that she might be a plant by Imperium, but why?

The female private was combing the little girl's hair after her bath. "I had a little sister about your age," the private said. "I loved to brush her hair and braid it. May I braid your hair?"

The little girl smiled and nodded.

"I'm Cura," said the private.

"Caussa," replied the little girl, sheepishly.

Cura completed a simple French braid in her hair. The girl was given some clothes and shoes that showed significant wear, but they were clean, and they fit. Caussa reach for Cura's hand as they exited the shower room, heading to meet Dr. Condoleo.

Dr. Condoleo was one of the psychologists employed by Initium Novum. She was a shorter woman, in her mid-forties. She was slender with long blond hair and sparkling blue eyes. Her smile was warm and inviting as the two of them walked up to meet her in the corridor.

"It is wonderful to meet you. I am Amibile," she said.

"This is Caussa," said Cura.

"Well, hello, Caussa. That is such a beautiful name. Would you come into my office and sit with me?"

Caussa drew closer to Cura and gripped tighter on her arm and hand.

"It's okay, she is coming too."

"I am?"

"You got her to speak, so yes, you are coming," Dr. Condoleo said quietly to Cura through her smile."

"I am," Cura reassured Caussa.

"General Depravo?" A voice came over the intercom. "Download is complete, sir. Sending you the data."

Depravo's screen lit up with a 3-D model of the outline of the base beneath Flat Top Mountain. A red beacon flashed showing the exact location of their "package" as it moved through the corridors, expanding the model as she went.

"Captain! In my office!" Depravo released the intercom button on his desk.

"Right away, sir."

The captain knocked and entered.

"Tell me everything you know about Flat Top Mountain," Depravo said as his gaze did not leave the floating image.

"It is a perfect place for a military base. The peak is over ten thousand feet, with a prominence of five thousand feet. It is within a range of mountains separating two valleys. It will be nearly impossible to sneak up on the hangar entrance to their base, as it is at the point of prominence, with lookout points on the far side, the top, and to the forward."

The captain stepped forward to use the model for reference as he continued.

"There are two primary modes of entrance. One is the long elevator shaft our package went down from their hangar. The second is a vehicle entrance at the base of the mountain on the south side. With our package inside, we now know it goes for several hundred yards. Both entrances are heavily guarded and are equipped with ground to air defense systems."

"Is there a third entrance?"

"Not really an entrance, but our infrared scanners detected an exhaust flume here." The captain pointed to a point near the top of the peak, about fifty yards down from the rear lookout point.

"The thermal imaging from our high-altitude drones with new data from our package gives us an idea that the channel is likely at a thirty-degree angle and several hundred yards long. It likely has a ladder of some sort used as an emergency exit, if needed."

"So, what's the problem, Captain?"

"The problem is the fans that are running." He zoomed in on the exhaust fume to show three areas with a difference in temperatures between them. "We believe these are a series of fans that help to push the exhaust out the long shaft. They appear to run in three shifts, ensuring that there is always air movement outward, while allowing each set downtime for potential maintenance. There is always a fan set running. If we were able to shut them all down, it would send an alarm. It would be like ringing a doorbell."

"Then that is exactly what we will do, Captain."

CAPITULUM XVII
(CHAPTER 17)

"Chief! Two minutes out!" the pilot shouted back to the cargo area of the craft.

Saxum unbuckled and walked toward the cockpit. "Excellent. Anything on radar?"

"Nothing, sir."

The aircraft was slowing to hover above an abandoned multilevel, open-air parking structure that was used for travelers at the Los Angeles airport. Sections of the structure had collapsed, caved in, and eroded over the years from war, extreme weather, and vandalism.

Alex walked up behind Chief Saxum and peered over his shoulder. "A busted-up LAX parking structure? I thought this was supposed to be secret," he said sarcastically.

"Sometimes the biggest secrets are hidden in plain sight," replied Saxum.

"Phoenix Nest, this is India November One, requesting access to land, over?" the pilot said into his commlink.

"Roger, India November One, Phoenix Nest has cleared you for landing on Pad Alpha, over?"

"Roger, Pad Alpha, out."

The craft slowly descended onto a pad in front of a hangar. The thrusters roared to life again, as it slowed its descent to a soft landing on the tarmac.

"Just what I need, another fucking hangar," Alex said beneath his breath.

The rear hatch opened to a team of doctors and soldiers. The chief stepped outward and shouted out commands to those awaiting orders. "Take these hospital beds to the medical wing, carefully. I don't want a hair harmed on any of them."

"Roger." The reply came from one of the soldiers.

"Doc, meet your new team." Saxum waved his hand toward the team of men and women in lab coats. "Take Alex here with you to the lab. Begin working immediately. I need my team back, pronto."

The chief looked to the medical staff. "Take the good doc here and this guy down to the lab. He is now your chief medical officer."

The team ushered Alex and Inquisitio out of the plane and into the hangar. They followed the convoy of hospital beds to a large thirty-by-thirty-foot platform. Once everyone was on the platform, one of the soldiers went over to a small control panel and pushed a button. The platform began to descend into the ground below. As Alex watched the horizon disappear, he could see the ground crew pulling the aircraft into the hangar.

Alex looked up to see two large plates begin to close together above them as they slowly lowered. Lights turned on above and around them as the large plates connected overhead. Thick gray concrete surrounded their platform as they sank deeper into the earth. Conduit connecting the lights and pipes lined the walls like an old-fashioned circuit board. The cement shaft opened into a large underground cargo bay with vehicles, aircraft, supply boxes, cargo nets, and weapons as far as his eyes could see. A few hundred yards to their front was a wall of glass separating them from a control room and large corridor that disappeared out of sight. The platform dropped a few hundred feet before resting on solid ground. The glass doors opened to the corridor, and they all made their way forward.

"Welcome to Phoenix Nest," the chief said as they entered the corridor. "I will come check on all of you after I debrief the commanding officer." Chief Saxum diverted toward the control room while Alex and Inquisitio followed the beds and medical team toward the medical wing of the base.

An unmarked supply truck drove up to the guard station to the supply tunnel at Flat Top Mountain.

"Papers?" the guard said as the truck stopped. The driver pulled out a shipping log that the guard looked over. He compared it to his supply log for the day. He looked back to the driver. "I don't see you on the list for today."

"Must have fallen off." The driver shrugged his shoulders and looked as if it was a common occurrence. "I got perishable food in here. You don't want it, fine, I will take it to another location. Doesn't bother me one way or another."

The guard looked at him and the truck for a few moments, nodded his head, and waved him through. He radioed to the loading dock to expect the truck.

Dr. Condoleo, Cura, and Caussa walked the corridors of Flat Top Mountain to ease her fear and better acquaint her with her surroundings. As they walked and pointed things out to Caussa, her grip on Cura's hand slowly lessened.

They turned a corner and entered a large bay. The bay was full of children. Some were playing on their cots, some playing on the floor with others. For the number of children in the room, it was relatively quiet.

Dr. Condoleo leaned down to speak softly to Caussa. "These are children who have been separated from their families, like you. It is okay if you are shy at first. We have a cot for you. Would you like to see it?"

They slowly walked to an empty cot about a third of the way into the room. It had a neat pillow, sheet, and blanket. At the head of the cot was a small footlocker. Caussa scanned the room slowly with an uneasy yet curious look on her face. Her hand slowly dropped from Cura's.

The two guards at the lookout point above the exhaust flume were joking as they scanned their sectors looking for any potential attack.

"Fifteen more minutes until we are relieved," one said to the other.

"Can't wait to grab some grub and hit the rack," the other replied as he stretched his arms over his head and let out a large yawn.

A small drone dropped down from above the roof of their post and began to hover in front of him, above the exhaust flume.

"Oh, fuck!" he said right before the drone opened fire, killing them both before they could sound the alarm.

The drone opened a bottom hatch to let a small charge drop into the flume.

A large blast was heard right before the room began to shake. Dust and debris fell from the ceiling; lights flickered then went off. The emergency lights kicked on and a high-pitched alarm began crying out. Red strobe lights began to flash, and a voice came over the intercom.

"Evacuate! Evacuate! This is not a drill, I repeat, this is not a drill. Calmly find your way to the nearest exit. This is not a drill. Evacuate. Evacuate!"

"Private, help me with all the children." Dr. Condoleo stood up. "Children, just like we practiced. Line up, two-by-two. Find your buddy. We are going to stay calm. We are going to stay together. Follow me. Private, please be the rear of our buddy line."

Dr. Condoleo led the group down the corridors to the stairwell that led down to the supply truck entrance at the base of the mountain. The children flinched and tensed at each soldier running past and every after shock.

An officer ran up to Dr. Condoleo. "What's going on, Lieutenant?" the doctor asked.

"An explosion in the exhaust tunnel. Not sure what caused it. Get those kids out of here quickly."

Dr. Condoleo nodded and continued her path.

"General Depravo, the strike was successful. Flat Top is evacuating. Awaiting orders," the captain said over the intercom.

"Send them in. I want everything from that lab. Destroy anything that gets in the way."

The back of the unmarked van burst open as a team of Imperium soldiers blasted their way into the corridor.

The team moved quickly and effectively through the corridors like a well-oiled machine, taking out every soldier with a weapon before they had a chance to respond.

Two members provided coverage at the lab entrance, while the others searched the lab for their intended packages.

"Captain, this is the team leader. We are in the lab. There is nothing here, sir. I repeat, the packages are gone. Over."

Depravo was listening in on the radio chatter from his office.

"Take what is avail—"

The captain's response was interrupted. "What do you mean there is nothing there?" Depravo shouted over the airwaves.

"Sir, the lab is empty, no computers, no lab equipment. It has been completely cleared."

Depravo angrily pushed everything off his desk. He stood up and threw his chair across the room. The veins in his neck and face began to bulge as his face reddened with rage. He grabbed the underside of his desktop and flipped the desk over onto the floor. He tilted his head back to let out a primal roar as every muscle in his body tightened. He reached through the mess on the floor to grab the commlink. "Kill them all. All of them! Destroy *everything!*"

Chief Saxum was debriefing the Initium Novum commanding officer, General Potestas in his office adjacent to the control room.

A young officer burst through the door. "Sir! Flat Top is under attack."

The general ushered him in.

"There was an explosion in the exhaust tunnel. A team of Imperium soldiers infiltrated the base. Major causalities. Radar shows more Imperium forces on the way. There are hundreds of noncombatants; families, children, service employees, with no one to protect them."

"Have they taken out our cargo craft?" the chief asked.

"Not yet, sir."

Chief Saxum spoke up. "We must bring them here, sir. We are the closest allied base. We cannot mobilize a unit to go defend fast enough. We can get them on those birds and get them in the air. They are sitting ducks right now."

"I agree, go take the CON," the general responded.

Saxum darted over to the control room. "Launch Bravo and Charlie Teams; have Delta on deck. Evacuate Flat Top, women, and children first. Use whatever birds are available. Have them use a scatter pattern and provide the coordinates once two hundred miles out. We need to give the fighters time to engage. We need to keep this location safe for as long as possible."

"Roger." The communications team was sending the orders out.

"Kyrie Eleison," the chief said under his breath as he watched the monitors.

Dr. Inquisitio pulled the memory drive from his coat pocket. He plugged it into the computer and pulled up a video file. "Before we dive deep into this, I wanted to show you this first."

Alex watched as Inquisitio pushed the Play button and stood back to give Alex room.

"Alex, Mary…" His father and mother were sitting at his childhood kitchen table. They were wearing the outfits they had on the day they were captured. They both looked solemn and tearful. He could see the TV behind them on the news channel, the natural light coming in from the window behind them, he and his sister out in the front yard playing. His parents had barely begun talking, and tears began to form in his eyes.

"I hope you will be at a point where you can at least understand the message we are trying to share," his father started, but got choked up.

His mother took over. "We have created something very wonderful. It's a vaccine, a way to use visium and vigorium to cure diseases and health issues that have plagued our civilization for decades. The data on this chip can save the world." His mother became tearful as her passion flooded her emotionally.

"That is why it is crucial this does not fall into the wrong hands," his father continued. "This very vaccine can also become a doomsday devise and end human life as we know it. We were supposed to begin human trials, but it is too late. Imperium has seized some of our coworkers already. It is a matter of time before we…" He trailed off, looked at his wife, and took a deep breath.

"It's okay, honey," she replied, patting the top of his hand. "If they are watching this, then it has already happened."

His father gave a nod and turned back to the camera. "We hope that we can get all of us out in time, but if you are watching this, it means we have been captured. This means the world's survival is now in your hands. I am so very sorry that this tremendous burden has fallen to you." Both his mother and father began crying.

"Find any Initium Novum person you can and get this chip to them. Tell them who you are. They will take good care of you. We love you both so very much." His father started sobbing as his mother reached forward and turned the video off.

Alex wiped the tears from his own eyes as he turned to face the doctor. "Okay, let's do this."

"I am going to take some blood for lab tests and put you in the body scanner. I want to run those samples against the samples I have collected from the team and my family. I am going to compare it to the vials of the vaccine that I have made. We need to figure out what makes you so special."

"I told you, Doc, I am not special."

Inquisitio hesitated, took a breath, and approached him. "There is something special about you, Alex, whether you believe it or not. There is a reason you are awake, and the rest aren't. Let's find out what that is."

CAPITULUM XVIII
(CHAPTER 18)

Cura and a handful of remaining soldiers were holding off the advancing Imperium team with their rifles as the cargo ships began to land. They had pulled their van out from the tunnel and were slowly moving in on the remaining survivors, who had been pinned in an alcove at the base of the mountain. The gunners on board the cargo ships were laying down suppressive fire while Dr. Condoleo and the children boarded the craft. After the crafts filled up, they ascended to begin flying in various directions.

Their craft's crew chief locked his weapon on the team of Imperium soldiers. Those who were not killed by the intense rapid fire were killed by the explosion of their supply truck when the gunner laid into it.

"Chief, all cargo birds are airborne," one of the controllers called out.

"What's the ETA of our fighters?"

"Two minutes," the controller replied.

"What's the ETA of the Imperium fighters?"

"Fifty seconds."

"Team leaders, get a move on," the chief ordered. "Those cargo ships are no match for their cruisers. Hurry up!"

"Roger, Chief," the team leaders responded.

"Cargo ships, evasive maneuvers. Fighters are on their way."

Cura took up a position on the opposite side of the gunner, out the side door. She could see the Imperium cruisers quickly approaching.

"Resist the urge to fire until they are closer, Private," the crew chief said over the headset. "I will try to draw them to my side. You look out for opportunities to get them as they pass by."

Cura looked inside the cargo bay at the frightened faces of the children. She took a deep breath and pulled her rifle up to her eye and waited.

Chief Saxum got on the radio. "Extraction team, keep on your current headings as much as possible. Separate the cruisers. It will be easier to take them down if they are separated."

———————

Depravo was in the Imperium control room watching over the monitors as the cruisers approached Flat Top Mountain.

"Thirty seconds to target," one of the pilots sent over the radio. "Cargo craft are taking off. Requesting permission to engage."

"Destroy everything. No survivors," Depravo answered back.

"Roger, locking on target," the team leader reported back.

Captain Sectator pulled General Depravo over to the side. "Sir, with all due respect, the tracker on the girl is still working. Would it not be wiser to allow them to take her wherever they are going? They may be going to the same base they took the research to. It could be a true chance to get it back, sir."

Depravo shot the captain a disgruntled look. He hated that the man was right. He gave the captain a nod and went back to the controllers.

"Cease fire!" Depravo said over the radio. "Do not engage the cargo ships. Take out the mountain."

"Roger," the team leaders repeated as they disengaged from the ships and turned on the mountain.

———•———

"What the fuck are they up to?" The chief rubbed his chin in awe as the cruisers stopped tailing the cargo ships and turned back to the mountain. "Team leaders, provide security for our cargo ships. The mountain has fallen. Let them shoot it up for target practice. Do not engage until engaged."

It was an uneasy and nerve-racking flight as each cargo craft and escort team flew in a different direction until out of range of the Imperium fleet. The chief gave the go ahead to provide their coordinates to the teams. He anxiously watched each of them, all the way in.

———————•

Alex nervously paced the lab while Dr. Inquisitio reviewed his lab work. The doctor made random grunts and noises as he took notes. He lifted his head up from the computer screen, rubbed his eyes, and then lifted his arms over his head in a long stretch and yawn.

"Let's take a break, Doc. Go grab some coffee, take a walk."

Inquisitio nodded in agreement. He stood up and they walked out into the corridor.

"What are you seeing?" Alex asked as they began to walk.

"Nothing remarkable yet. The markers in your system appear to match the markers in the vaccine I made. I reviewed the data on the chip with my own, and they are spot on. I am missing something. I know I am. There must be something there."

"What if there isn't, Doc? What if it is just a random abnormality? What if I truly am just an average Joe?"

"Do you remember if you or your family had any kind of chronic conditions? Any serious infections, anything like that?"

"My memory is still pretty fuzzy, thanks to your little experiments," Alex replied.

"Think about it some more, will you?"

The two walked into the cafeteria and grabbed some food off the serving line and sat down at a table to eat. Alex looked down at his plate and picked up a roll. "Now that I think about it, we never had bread in the house. I didn't eat my first roll until I was in the training camp." Alex bit into the roll, closed his eyes, and savored the bite.

"No bread? Did someone have a glucose issue?"

Alex thought for a while. He closed his eyes and tried to draw any memory involving bread. A memory of a conversation he had with his mother in their kitchen popped up.

"Why can't I have a doughnut?" the young Alex asked.

"Your body cannot handle it, Alex. I am so sorry. But when you eat things like breads, pastries, and things, you become anemic," his mother replied.

"What's anemic?"

"Iron is an essential mineral in our blood. When you have too little iron in your bloodstream, it is called anemia. Eating foods like bread cause you to have too little iron in your blood, and that can lead to serious issues, honey," his mother said compassionately.

Alex opened his eyes. "I was anemic as a child."

The doctor dropped his fork mid bite. "That's it!" He shot up from his seat and raced to the lab.

"Doc, wait up. What's it?" Alex said as he raced after him.

"Your iron levels in your blood look perfect. Too perfect. You were anemic, until your parents gave you the vaccine. It began to work in your body to remove your intolerance of gluten. But you are not cured. The vaccine is consistently working in your body to keep your iron levels stable. The vaccine worked on the Black Death like it is working on that roll you just ate. If my theory is correct, I bet the iron in everyone else is at a toxic level. It didn't show up in their lab work because the vaccine is trying to fight it off. We are supplying iron in the nutrition we are providing them. It is too much for the vaccine to handle."

Doctor Inquisitio drew up syringes for each of the patients still in a coma. He provided each another injection. "I am going to hold off on the nutrition and just keep them on Lactated Ringer's for now. With a booster of the vaccine and no additional iron provided, it should be enough to wake them."

"I don't understand, Doc. You mean the Black Death is still inside them, inside me?"

"Not any longer. The booster was enough to overpower the replication of Black Death inside you. The others are in a deadlock, so to speak. The iron provided in the nutrition bags was too much iron for the vaccine to handle. It is keeping the Black Death at bay but cannot process the amount of iron in their systems. Boosting their vaccine and removing the iron should be enough to overpower the Black Death inside them."

"For everyone's sake, I hope you are right."

Up above on the tarmac, the cargo ships landed to unload the survivors, Chief Saxum and a medical team was ready to assess and treat the wounded. The adjacent hangar became a medical bay. It was a space large enough to treat and assess. Cots were lined up in rows as the most critically injured were rushed to makeshift surgery areas while less severe cases were placed in the holding area.

Chief Saxum looked at the medical officer in charge. "Give me a status update in two hours. I want to move people underground as quickly as possible."

"You look uneasy, Chief," the medical officer replied.

"It was just too easy. Why did they decide not to engage? What happened?" The chief thought for a bit longer. "The girl! Where is that little girl that was found by our patrol? Did we scan her for a tracking device?"

"We scanned her arm in a typical routine. We destroyed the rags she was wearing."

"Scan her again, her whole body. Now!"

The medical officer ran off to the hangar to find Caussa. The medical officer briefed Dr. Condoleo on what was needed. She and Cura were able to talk Caussa into the scan.

"I will be by your side the whole time," Cura said to a nervous Caussa. Caussa nodded as they laid her on the exam table and began the scan.

At the base of her skull, right below her first cervical disc, was a tracking chip. "Get Chief Saxum up here stat," the medical officer said to the nurse. "We have a serious issue."

———

"Sir, we have their location," one of the controllers shouted out to General Depravo. He walked up behind his chair and peered over his shoulder.

"Where?" he asked.

"Old LAX, sir."

Depravo gave a small chuckle and smirk. "Excellent." He turned to the captain. "I want the key leaders in the war room in twenty minutes. Put all our mobile units and squadrons on standby. Use the last of the serum we have on as many adults as you can."

———•———

Alex sat beside Herrera's bed watching the monitors and looking for any movement. He hoped the doctor was right. He could not remember having a connection with anyone like the one he felt with Herrera. He could not deny the longing he had since they first met.

He was uncomfortably reclined in a chair, about to drift off to sleep for a much-needed overdue nap. A small twitch of her hand and a quick jolt on her heart monitor grabbed his attention. He sprang up to the bedside, looking back and forth at the change in her heartbeat on the monitor and her body for additional movements.

She began adjusting her body as if she was uncomfortable and let out a few groans; however, her eyes did not open. Alex raced out of the room to find Dr. Inquisitio. Going room by room, he found the doctor in the room with one of his children who had awakened.

"Doc, Herrera is moving, but not awake. What does that mean?"

"It means our plan is working. I would like to introduce you to my son, Orion," the doctor replied.

"Hi, Orion, I am Alex."

"Hello, sir," the child responded wearily.

"He is the first to wake. My wife and the other children are stirring, like what you described for Herrera. I am sure it is just a matter of time before they wake."

Chief Saxum was in the room with the medical officer, Dr. Condoleo, Cura, and Caussa.

"Imperium changed where they are placing the trackers. It is right at the base of the skull. It is perfectly placed to be almost impossible to remove without causing paralysis or death."

"So they know where we are and made it virtually impossible for Caussa to have a normal life. What are our options? Can we turn it off, destroy it without hurting this poor child?" the chief asked.

"Removal is the riskiest. Given the position, I am leery of doing anything to it. The smallest of movements could be life threatening."

"Okay, keep thinking on that. They know where we are. It is just a matter of time before an attack. Get everyone inside. We will continue the exams and checks where it is safer."

CAPITULUM XIX
(CHAPTER 19)

Chief Saxum walked into the medical wing of the compound to find Alex pacing in the hallway.

"How is everything going?" the chief asked as he met eyes with Alex.

"Doc is in with his kiddos. They are awake and responding well. His wife and the team are showing signs of life but have not wakened."

"That is amazing news. What was the secret?"

"Iron. You will have to get with the doc for the specifics on that."

"How are you doing?"

"All right, I guess. It is both relieving and disappointing to know that I am not 'special.' While the weight of that thought was overwhelming and nothing that I wanted, the hope that I could be a key in ending all this bullshit was…motivating."

The chief took a step closer. "You are the key, Alex. Maybe not in the way you thought. Without you, we would not have the chip your parents left you, we would not have this vaccine, we wouldn't be saving my team and the doc's family right now—"

Alex interrupted. "The team wouldn't have been captured if not for me. They wouldn't have been tortured. Sanator would not be dead."

"Last time I checked, you weren't a psychic. There is no way to predict what would not have happened without you. What did happen is we have a vaccine that can help end this shit. We have you. You have proved to be a valuable asset to our cause."

"I didn't ask for this. I didn't want this. Sanator—"

The chief interrupted. "Sanator knew he could possibly give his life for our cause. He was willing to make that sacrifice. Now you can decide if his death was in vain or not. You helped get us to this point. You feel responsible? Then do something about it. I have an open slot on Herrera's team. I have a craft that needs a pilot." The chief slapped him in the chest.

"I am not a soldier," Alex said in a stern tone.

"I don't fucking care," the chief said. "You have skills that you learned. You are a tough son of a bitch. You are tactically sound. You are a survivor, and whether or not you believe it, you fucking care about others. I don't give a fuck whether you wear a uniform or not. I need you on my team. The ball is in your court. Let me know what you decide."

The chief brushed past Alex on his way to speak with Dr. Inquisitio. He paused and looked back at Alex. "Sooner than later." The chief turned back around and walked off.

Dr. Inquisitio rounded a corner and accidentally bumped into the chief. "Just who I was looking for. My kids, my wife, and Herrera are awake. The others are all starting to gain consciousness."

"Great, take me to them," responded the chief.

"Me too," Alex said.

The chief made his rounds to see all the teammates, one by one. They were all given the brief overview of what the last several days had entailed but were encouraged to rest and recover.

"What do you think recovery time is, Doc?" asked the chief.

"I really have no idea. This is unknown territory we are in. They will need a full workup done, physical, lab work, physical therapy, occupational therapy, strengthening; I really have no clue. It will most likely be on an individual basis. Typical recovery time is six to eight weeks."

"We have hours, Doc. Days at best. Imperium knows we are here. It is a matter of time before they attack. I need my best team fit for duty."

"I understand, and they need time to recover. Their bodies have been through hell. I can't in good conscience release them until they have had a psych eval as well…"

"Make it happen, Doc." The chief turned around to Alex. "I need an answer."

"I haven't one to give, Chief."

The chief looked back and forth between Alex and Dr. Inquisitio for a moment. He took a deep breath. "We simply don't have enough soldiers to defend ourselves for long. This is my best team, my alpha team. I need them.

We need them. This is likely to be our last stand." The chief paused a moment more.

"Alex, come with me. I have something I want to show you. Doc, give me an update in an hour."

Chief Saxum and Alex took off down the corridor. They walked deep into the far side of the base to a corridor that ended at a large metal door. It had triple identification authorization and Authorized Personnel Only in large black letters. The chief looked into a retina scanner, said his name, and placed his thumb on a scanner simultaneously. A large metal click could be heard as the door unlocked and opened.

———————•———————

Depravo had his top five military leaders in the war room with the captain at his side.

One of the officers spoke up. "Sir, with all due respect, why are we sending everyone? This goes against every military strategy I know. I feel it is narrow-sighted and could cause grave consequences in the long run."

"They killed our board members, General. They stole our research. I want this war to end permanently. I have no doubt they will be expecting us, so we need to ensure there is no way they can win. We will overwhelm them with firepower."

Another officer spoke up. "That is lunacy. They wouldn't be expecting us in large capacity if not for your circus of a display at Flat Top. Not to mention this secret squadron you created without including any of us, only to have the crafts recklessly used and destroyed. I am appalled that the board put up with your shenanigans as long as they did. The only reason you are in that chair now is that there is no one to remove you."

Depravo held back the inner rage pulsating through his veins. Taking a deep breath, he relaxed his fists from the white-knuckled balls hidden by his gloves. "Is that how you really feal?"

The officer nodded.

"How you all feel?"

All but the captain nodded.

"Okay then." Depravo pushed a button on the keyboard in front of him. A security force team burst into the room. "Guards, throw these men in the brig for attempted mutiny."

"This is outrageous." One said.

"You can't do this," said another.

The guards, slightly confused, looked at General Depravo, then at the captain by his side, then at the group of leaders, hands on their sidearms.

The captain looked at Depravo, then to the leaders, then to the guards.

"Captain, think about what he is doing, Think about your career," one pleaded.

"I am. Guards! Your commanding general gave you an order," the captain belted out.

"Yes, sir! Sorry, sir!" the team leader replied. He ushered in his team with weapons drawn. "Gentlemen, you are under arrest for attempted mutiny. Stand up slowly, hands raised above your heads."

"I am going to fucking kill you," one said in anger as he was handcuffed.

"I have heard that a lot lately, and yet here I am," replied Depravo mockingly.

The men were all bound and removed from the war room.

Depravo turned to the captain. "Congratulations. You have just received a field promotion, Colonel Sectator."

"It's an honor, sir. I have known nothing but war, for as long as I can remember. I am ready to end this. You have all their key leaders and most of their fighting force in one location. Mass destruction blasted on every monitor and screen. The remaining few will have no choice but to surrender or die."

"Glad we are on the same page, Colonel. Now we have much to do. Assemble everyone out on the yard. I will address them, and then we will end this."

Chief Saxum walked Alex into a large bay area. There were engineers, technicians, and other support staff working vigorously on a large bowl-shaped structure in the center of the room. It was roughly six feet high along the outer rim, with a fifty-foot diameter. It had the color and texture of vigorium metal that plated its exterior.

The chief motioned Alex forward as he began speaking. "We have been working on a prototype aircraft for several years. Our lightest, most agile, fastest craft yet. Until you arrived, we have not been able to get it fully functional."

Alex gave a perplexed look. "Seriously?"

"We didn't have the data on visium and vigorium that we needed to make these crafts unstoppable. That data from your chip transformed this project, and within the last several days, we have made tremendous strides getting them up and running.

Herrera and her team helped with the design and testing of these crafts until they were shot down on that patrol several months ago. Once they are fit for duty with the new technology, we can get these flying. With the imminent threat of attack, we need to get this project completed. That is where you come in."

"Chief, I still—"

"Hold your thought. I want you to join my team, yes, but this is a different request. You flew Imperium's new craft. You know its capabilities, its inner workings. I need you to sit down with my design team and tell them absolutely everything you remember about that experience. We can learn from it, grow from it. Make our crafts as indestructible as possible."

The chief studied Alex's face while he listened and thought about what he was saying, waiting for a sign of confirmation. "Please, Alex."

"Yeah, sure. Let's do it," Alex said reluctantly.

"First let me show you what we have so far." The chief walked Alex to a rolling metal ladder on the side of the structure. He walked Alex up to the top, where the bowl concaved slightly onto a platform.

Long metal plates formed the walking surfaces and gave it the appearance of an old wagon wheel. The walkable spaces were grated metal that consisted of the outer ring, eight "spokes" that led to the inner circle in the middle. A small control panel was placed at the end of each spoke near the outer circle. In between the walkways, were pie-slice-shaped pads with markings in the middle of a circle where someone would stand. Each of the pads were translucent with a dull blue light glowing from underneath.

The chief walked to the closest control panel. "Alex, welcome to Phoenix Nest, Alpha." The chief put his hand on the control panel to confirm his fingerprints. A screen rose up with a full-body picture of Chief Saxum, his demographics and credentials.

The center circle moved a one-eighth turn. A metal click sounded as it unlocked and began to rise. A metal cylinder rose the center, roughly six feet higher than the platform. It was lined with spherical holes from top to bottom in columns that aligned with each of the platforms. The holes were about the size of a bowling ball. It looked to Alex like a bunch of creepy eye sockets on some sort of robotic space alien.

"This is the future of warfare. No longer needing large hangars to store aircraft and large tarmacs to take off and land. With these nests we can store forty-eight aircraft. We can launch eight simultaneously in six intervals that are literally seconds apart. Within two minutes we can have all forty-eight airborne."

"I will admit, that is super impressive." Alex sounded astounded.

"Okay, let's meet with the design team.

CAPITULUM XX
(CHAPTER 20)

General Depravo and Colonel Sectator were up on the roof of the building, looking into a yard full of Imperium soldiers and employees. He smiled to himself, as they were nothing more to him than ants. He chuckled at the thought that he was standing right where he had killed each of the board members. How he hated the indignant and ignorant! How he had longed for a moment like this, to gain supremacy, to rule the word.

"Colonel Sectator, how are we coming on our new soldiers?" Depravo asked.

"Moving along well, sir. I took the remaining serum to the lab so that we could begin the production of more. It is in the process of being made as we speak. I had enough left to make twenty new soldiers who are now being cleared medically."

"Excellent work, Colonel. How long before we have more serum ready?"

"The scientists believe they will have a batch that can transform one hundred soldiers by tomorrow, sir."

"After this speech, ready our forces. I need you to remain here and run the facility. I am going to the mobile command center. I want to be on site when Initium Novum crumbles. Make sure this is broadcast on every screen and monitor. It's time to end the resistance once and for all. It's time to make history."

Depravo walked up to a microphoned platform that overlooked the yard. He waved at the adoring crowd below him with a politician's grin as he began his speech. "Imperialists! Today we embark on the final chapter of this war. It is time to end the treasonous acts from those who would resist law and order.

"These villains are responsible for the death of our beloved council members. These criminals have insinuated violence and destruction. These anarchists have pushed their evil agenda on the world for long enough."

Depravo gave dramatic pause for the crowd to respond.

Shouts of anger in alignment with his words rose over the barbed wire fence into the surrounding forest. Once pleased with the response, he continued with false humility. "I hear your cries for justice. Please do not take matters into your own hands. Now is the time to pledge your allegiance to this great organization and to me. We have superior technology that will make us an unstoppable force. We have a new serum that will make you invincible."

Depravo help up the last remaining vial of Black Death.

"This serum is safe and effective. It has been battle tested to make you stronger, sharper, and faster than ever before. You won't have to worry about fatigue or exhaustion. Making the wrong decision will be a thing of the past. This super serum is the key to finally fulfilling our destiny."

He held the vial up in triumph as the masses of soldiers and imperium employees cheered.

"It is with great sadness that I share with you that this vial is the last of the serum. The evil forces of Initium Novum stole our research for their wicked ways."

Boos echoed off the walls of the buildings within the compound.

"This is why we need as many of you who are able bodied to volunteer to lead this attack to get back what is rightfully ours. Only a few of you will have the honor of using the last of this serum in the upcoming battle. Fear not! We *will* make more; we *will* become the superpower this world needs. Join me, and you will never have a single worry, ever again."

The crowd erupted in praise and applause as Depravo looked around and waved at everyone. He stepped down from the podium and pulled Sectator aside. "Compile a small unit to help with processing new recruits. Be selective on the serum. Choose those who normally would not pass training, the most expendable. We just need their vessels, not their minds." Depravo shot a devil's grin. "The smart and strong ones will lead our ground forces. The drones will fly our new crafts."

Sectator jotted notes and nodded his head in agreement. "What is our timetable for roll out?"

"Tentative forty-eight hours. That should be enough time to have more serum made to fill all fifty of our aircrafts. That should give you enough time to weaponize the new recruits and get them fitted for battle. You will stay back here, continuing to recruit new soldiers and overseeing the hangar and flight crew. I am going out in the mobile command center to lead from the battle site."

"Sir, with all due respect, we cannot afford to lose you in battle. I volunteer to lead this mission for you."

"Sectator, so loyal. No, I need to be there, to show the troops we lead from the front, to be able to make quick decisions and adjust fire as needed. I need you here, to run this whole operation for me. After this war is over, this will all be yours to run."

Sectator's eyes widened, and a pirate smile grew from his chin. "It will be my honor, sir. I will not fail you."

"I know. Now go. Update me on your progress."

Sectator turned to head for the elevator doors.

Depravo looked around at the mass of people shuffling to head toward the hangar to enlist. He chuckled. He was finally getting what he wanted. Even in his narcissism, he was surprised at how he was able to pull this off. Once he regained control of both the vaccine and the serum, there would never be another force large enough or strong enough to overthrow him.

———•———

Alex was joined by Probus, Pares, and Ferox to consult with the design team of the new defender aircraft. "Where's Herrera?" Alex asked.

"She is still coming around," replied Pares. "Let's get to work."

Each of them described the feelings, sensations, and thoughts from their time under Imperium's control. They shared their perspectives on the cruiser's agility, speed, and power. They shared their ideas for improvements and ways in which the new defenders could overtake the cruisers.

Pares stretched his arms over his head and let out a yawn. "Let's take a breather. We have been at this for hours. Go grab coffee, food, whatever. Be back in an hour."

The design team, Ferox, and Probus all stood and exited.

Pares grabbed Alex by the shoulder to hold him back. "Herrera is having a tough time. She hasn't really spoken to anyone since she woke up and has not gotten out of bed. I told the team that she was still adjusting, but something else is wrong. Maybe she would talk to you."

"You sure?"

Pares gave a sigh. "Look, I know you care for her. I still don't like you, but it's not anything you've done. You have proven yourself to my team and appear to be a decent guy. I don't like you because of what you represent." He took another deep breath. "Maybe because you are not a subordinate of hers, maybe because she may have other feelings for you. Whatever the reason, she will not talk to us. Please, the team needs her. Initium Novum needs her."

Alex gave a nod and began walking back to the medical wing of the compound. He passed a room full of children playing. One little girl caught his eye. It was the little girl brought into the hangar at Flat Top, before they took off. She was laughing and jumping to a silly song that the group was listening to. Within a short time, she went from scared and uncommunicative to laughing and playing.

He smiled in spite of himself. How he longed to have that kind of resiliency, that kind of innocence and purity of spirit. He also ached for her life moving forward. Her parents were most likely dead, and she would have to experience life without them. While he could relate, he was hopeful she would never experience the upbringing he was forced to endure.

The rage within him deepened toward Imperium, thinking of all the innocence lost within its walls, all the lives ruined. This little girl has already experienced so much trauma and grief. All these children had. It needed to end. A single tear rolled down his cheek as he turned and continued down the hall to see Herrera.

Herrera was reclined in her hospital bed with her head turned away from the door when Alex walked in. He gave a few small knocks on the door frame as he entered. She did not respond. He walked around and took a seat in the chair near the wall where she was staring.

He sat awhile in silence, seeing if she would even make eye contact. She let out a sigh as she turned away from Alex, to lie on her side facing the opposite wall.

After a few more minutes, Alex finally spoke up. "I don't know what is circling in your head right now, but I imagine it is all the shit we have been through lately. I don't know what to say, so I am just going to sit here and be here. If you want to talk, that's cool. If you don't, that is cool too. All I will say is your team is worried about you…and so am I."

After several more minutes, Herrera responded. "I failed my team."

"No, you didn't. How?"

"They saw me give up. They saw me break. They saw me get violated in plain sight and not fight back. I just…" Herrera began to sob. "I couldn't…I…"

Alex got up and walked around the bed to squat down in front of her. He gently placed a hand on her arm. With his other hand he brushed her hair back from her face.

"You did *not* fail your team. All of us were violated, tortured, and punished. That sick son of a bitch wanted another reaction from you. He got off on that sick shit. Your team does not think any less of you. They care about you. They need you."

Herrera began shaking her head as she continued crying. "I can't. That bastard broke me. I caved in front of my team…"

"We all broke. Depravo made damn sure we all did. How else could he have done what he did to us, placing that curse on us, making us his fucking puppets? He might as well of had his hand up our asses. In time we will all need to process the shit we went through. Right now, you need to pull all of that into anger and rage and make sure that asshole *never* does that again."

Herrera rolled to her back and looked up at the ceiling through tear-stained eyes. "I don't think I can."

Alex took a deep breath. "Will you come with me somewhere? I want to show you something."

Herrera locked eyes with Alex. Sincerity and compassion were pouring through his deep blue eyes. She searched for what felt like hours for any sign of malice or ill intent. The deeper she looked, the harder it was to look away. There was a genuineness about him she had not felt from anyone else. She felt it when they were in the prison together and felt it while they were held up in the house together. She couldn't help but trust him.

She finally held out her hand and sat up. He helped her as she fumbled a bit, weakened by the days of being bedridden. Once she gained some balance, he helped her out of the room and down the hall. They stopped at the room where Alex watched the children playing.

"I don't pretend to know what your childhood was like. I have no idea what you have experienced outside of the time I've known you. You have seen a window into my childhood. What I can tell you is what I have seen of you in that small amount of time. You have the resiliency that I see in these children. You are one tough, bad ass commanding officer. You are battle hardened, calculated, skilled, and deadly. You are also kind, compassionate, caring, and have a softness that I can't help but want to be around."

Alex stumbled finding words for a moment as he looked at her.

She turned to look into his eyes.

Finally, he was able to spit out, "I am going to join your team for now, to finish this thing."

"Then I guess we're screwed," Herrera said, emotionless.

Alex waited, trying not to be offended, until a small smile began to show at the side of her mouth.

Alex smiled back. He went to leave but hadn't realized he had been holding her hand the whole time they had been standing there. "Oh, uh, I, uh, need to get back, helping the design team, and uh, yeah."

Alex awkwardly turned to head back toward the hangar. He ran into crash carts and other objects against the hallway walls.

Herrera shot a blushing side smile and glance as he turned the corner.

Herrera stood for a while longer, watching the children play. It took her back to a time when she wasn't concerned with the war, before she lost her innocence. She thought back to when she first met Saxum. She couldn't let him down. She couldn't let her team down. She needed to compartmentalize the trauma for now. Depravo's reign needed to end. She walked back down the hall to get medically cleared for duty.

CAPITULUM XXI
(CHAPTER 21)

"Colonel, I need an update." Depravo was getting impatient. The bloodlust was welling inside him like a wolf tearing into the flesh of its prey after a fresh kill. He needed to inflict pain on his enemies.

"Sir, the last of the drones have been cleared for duty. We have each craft assigned and have recruited one thousand ground troops."

"Excellent! Send out the marching orders. We step out in twelve hours."

———————

Alpha team, Chief Saxum, and the design team were steady at work in the conference room within the secret hangar when Herrera walked into the room.

"Catch me up to speed," she said as she grabbed an open chair.

"You good, Ma'am?" Pares asked.

"Good enough."

The team worked through the next few hours finalizing the updates to the new phoenix defenders.

"Everyone, get some rest. We will unveil the defenders in eight hours. Let's pray you all will have time to test them before we are attacked." The chief yawned as he rubbed his eyes. It was midnight.

The team stood up and began walking back to their quarters. Each team had a pod that contained a common area in the center of their individual rooms. The pods were clustered in an area not far from the cafeteria.

"Who's up for some grub?" Ferox asked as they neared their pod.

"I could eat," said Probus.

"Me too," said Pares. "Bellator, Ma'am?"

"Nah, I am good," replied Alex. "See you all in the morning."

"I'm going to grab something to go," Herrera responded. "I'm pretty exhausted."

Alex walked to his room and shut the door behind him. He sat down at the small desk chair next to his bunk to disrobe. He slipped off his boots and socks and pulled his shirt off over his head. He stood back up to change into shorts for bed, when he caught his reflection in a standing mirror on the closet door. It had been a long time since he had looked at his reflection.

He moved his hand across the multiple scars on his bicep and across his chest and abdomen. He turned halfway around to look at the scars on his back. He got lost in horrible memories from his torture. A knock at his door nearly had him jump out of his skin. He gathered himself quickly and answered the door.

Herrera was waiting on the other side with a meal box from the cafeteria. "I, uh, didn't know if you, uh, might be hungry, so I, uh gabbed something for you." Herrera awkwardly held out the meal box, looking uneasy.

Alex stepped to the side, ushered her into his room, and shut the door behind her.

"So, about earlier…" Alex was rubbing the back of his head. "I, want to apologize if, I…"

Herrera put the box down on the desk and turned to him as he continued. She studied his face and body as he spoke. She hadn't paid attention to his body while they were being tortured, for obvious reasons. She took a small step toward him and reached out toward his chest.

Alex flinched at first, but the look in her eyes told him it was okay and that he was safe.

She ran her fingers across the multiple scars on his chest and abdomen. She was amazed at his resiliency as touching his scars deepened the understanding of all the horrors he had faced.

Somehow, despite all he had been through, he was still a warm and caring person. She could feel his heartbeat increase as she softly brushed across his chest, up toward his shoulders. She studied each line, tracing the outline of a broad, sculpted physique as if it were a crafted masterpiece unfolding in front of her.

She slowly moved her hands from his shoulders down to his biceps. She examined the scars from the trackers with the slightest touch of her fingers.

Alex raised both arms to Herrera's blouse and began unbuttoning it from the bottom. Their eyes locked while she allowed Alex to slip her blouse off over her shoulders and onto the floor. He watched as she crossed her arms to pull her undershirt up and over her head.

He reached out to touch the multiple scars she had gained from all she has endured. It amazed him how she was incredibly strong and yet incredibly soft and vulnerable. He had never met someone with such fortitude and passion.

Herrera grabbed his hand and led him to the bed. She guided him down on his back as she lay down next to him. She pushed her torso up onto her forearm as she caressed his chest and stomach. Her spellbound soul slipped deeper into his enchanting blue eyes.

He quivered slightly as her hand slid further down his abdomen to the waistband of his pants. She toyed with his waistline, running her fingers across the belt loops and fly of his pants. Rubbing down in between his legs, she grabbed the rock-hard bulge that had formed from her seductive fondling.

In unison they both slowly unbuttoned each other's pants, slowly pulling them down and off. Herrera sat up and slid her body up on top of Alex, straddling his groin. She pulled off her sports bra and slowly lowered herself onto his chest.

Alex wrapped his arms around her back as she laid her head onto his shoulder, with her face on his neck. The feel of her nervous breath on his neck sent chills down his spine as she caressed his hair and ear with her free hand. She moved her nose and lips up his neck, to his ears, and to the side of his face.

The smell of his skin was alluring as she lost herself further, drowning in the passion filling the air. The warmth of her soft, supple kiss on his cheek begged him to turn into her longing gaze. The volcano of suppressed desire erupted as their lips met for the first time.

Her hips began gyrating as she pressed her pelvis harder into his jock. His hand moved downward to pull her panties out of the way, finally sliding the last remaining piece of clothing dividing their two bodies off and away.

Their kisses deepened as their bodies melted into each other, hands kneading harder into each other as she slipped her hand downward, caressing the fully erect phallus. Using her hand, she guided him into her warm, welcoming secret garden.

Both let out a muffled grown of ecstasy as she slid down farther onto his throbbing appendage. The pounding of their heartbeats played out the rhythm and set the pace like a wild mating call. Their muscles tensed and bodies began spasming, building up to a climax that would topple the tallest peaks of the Himalayas.

Groans of intense satisfaction escaped from their mouths as their heavy breathing brought them down from their erotic high. Sweat dripped from their bodies as Herrera lay on top of Alex elated and exhausted.

"This is the best food delivery I have ever had," joked Alex.

Herrera punched him playfully in the ribs and smirked. "I better be getting a good tip," she replied.

"Then I guess it is time for round two." Alex rolled her over and slid back inside her.

The unwelcoming sound of the alarm woke them both from their deep sleep, bodies still entangled from the night's passion. They quickly gathered their clothes and slipped into the shower room. They hoped to sneak a few more minutes of intimacy before the reality of the day's events began.

The water ran down their enveloped bodies as they took turns pleasuring and washing each other.

"Will you two knock it off? *Jesus!*" Ferox's voice came through the other side of the shower curtain. "You kept me up all night."

"Watch how you talk to your commanding officer," Pares snapped back. "But seriously, enough."

The team met in the conference room after breakfast. Chief Saxum entered the room and sat down at the head of the table. "Okay, the presentation begins at 0800 hours. After my speech we will launch all of you up and out. Now, who has the honor of the first launch?"

Pares spoke up. "I think it should be Alex."

"Wow, I am honored and…shocked," replied Alex.

"Well, without you, we wouldn't be where we are now. You truly were the missing piece, and if something goes wrong, I would rather you get blown up instead of one of my team," joked Pares.

"Gee, thanks." Alex said as he smirked.

"All in favor?" the chief asked.

"I," said Probus.

"Hell yes," Ferox shouted.

Herrera looked up at Alex and locked eyes for a moment. "I," she said with a smile.

"Then so be it," Chief Saxum stated. Meet in the hangar and the base of the podium in thirty minutes. Dismissed."

CAPITULUM XXII
(CHAPTER 22)

The hangar was buzzing with life as all the walkways and stairways were crowded with those able to attend, eagerly awaiting the big reveal. Chief Saxum was reviewing his notes at the base of the nest. Alex was the last to arrive.

"Thought you were having second thoughts," Ferox said as Alex walked up to them.

"Just taking it all in, I suppose. I am not one to want to be in the spotlight, so this is—"

Herrera grabbed his arm. "Hey, you will do great. Just don't fuck it up," she said with a laugh.

"All right, ladies and gents, showtime," Chief Saxum said as he looked to the team before climbing the stairs. He walked to the podium and tested the feedback on the microphone. Once he got a clear sound, he began. "Thank you all for being here this morning as we enter a new beginning for humankind. For far too long, we have been under the oppressive thumb of Imperium Corporation, which has withheld common needs and resources from civilization to force obedience through suffering. Today is a new day. We finally have the missing piece to end this awful war with Imperium."

"Alex, that's your cue," Herrera said as she motioned him to the stairs. Alex made his way up to Chief Saxum's side slowly, taking in the massive number of people staring eagerly back at him.

"This gentleman here was able to secure the missing data we so desperately needed to complete our research on visium and vigorium. This gentleman gave us the key we needed to create more effective vaccines to reduce sickness and disease. This gentleman gave us a better understanding of these two precious metals to build a fighter craft that is more agile, faster, and superior in every way to Imperium's most impressive craft. May I have the pleasure to introduce to you, Alex Bellator."

The applause was deafening as it reverberated against the metal walls and ceiling.

Alex leaned over to the chief. "Laid it on just a bit thick, don't you think?"

"The people need something to believe in, and that's you, Alex. None of what I said is untrue."

The chief waved his arms to calm the audience so he could continue. "Without further ado, Alex has the honor to showcase Phoenix Nest."

The crowd erupted in applause as Alex stepped down from the podium and walked toward the launch pad. He pulled up his information on the control pad and watched as the cylinder rose from the center of the nest. Instead of empty eye sockets this time, there were orbs filling the cavities.

Alex stepped forward to accept the orb. Blue energy radiated from the seams and crevasses between the components making up the bowling-ball-sized energy source as it came to life. It floated free from the cylinder as if being pulled toward Alex. His arms outstretched toward the orb. As his fingers reached the dimples, the emanating blue light intensified, immersing the platform with a blinding brilliance so astounding that it instilled hope and pride in all who witnessed. In an instant the roar of applause became so silent a cricket could be heard in the background.

Five dimples on each side aligned with his fingertips. Alex lifted into the air as if being pulled by an invisible rope. The orb began morphing into a yoke, stemming outward as the Phoenix defender took shape. His body tilted backward as his torso and legs bent into a reclined, seated position, with the yoke between his legs.

A harness and helmet grew out of the seat as the cockpit took shape around him. Within seconds an elongated horizontal teardrop-shaped craft had completed its transformation. Had it not been for the glowing light around it, its light blue color would be difficult to see from the ground.

It flattened on both sides of the cockpit to form the leading edges of the wing. The nose cone elongated and flattened a yard in front of his feet. The rear of the craft rounded from both sides of the wing to an elongated oval that held the propulsion system.

The craft began slowly hovering forward as he viewed the whole complex from above. There was not a single piece of glass on the vessel, yet he could see all around him, as if he were suspended in a bubble. Inside the hangar he saw people shouting and cheering. Over in the broken-down parking structure, he could see refugees staring in disbelief.

A few moments later Herrera flew up next to him. She looked over with a smirk. "You think you can handle it?"

He smirked back. "Follow me." He moved the yoke forward, and the defender began a sharp decent. "Oh, shit!" He leveled the craft back out. "You better follow me, cupcake," Herrera said as she soared ahead of him. Pares and Ferox and Probus followed to the rear.

"Please try not to take us down this time, Bellator," Pares said sarcastically.

"The heads-up display follows your head and eye movements," she said as he pulled up behind her. "Range, horizon, speed, altitude; all right there. Scroll through each with pressure from your right fingertips."

He started moving his fingers to scroll through each of the displays.

"Your left fingertips control the weapon systems. Let's see your moves," she said as she began a simple barrel roll.

He followed suit. It felt as though his thoughts were in sync with the controls of the ship, like the ship knew what he wanted to do. No nasty goo filling his ear cavities this time. No one cramming data into his skull, either. Rolls, loops, twists, all being performed as though he were a veteran fighter pilot.

He looked out over the curvature of the earth and the horizon as the sun was setting. The mesmerizing purples, pinks, oranges, and yellows shot out from behind picture-painted clouds. The shadows cast onto the mountains below made them even more majestic and awe inspiring.

From this height, with this view, it was almost believable that God truly existed. The grandeur and magnificence of what was slowly passing below him was enough to engrave in his soul that some celestial deity was in control, that this rock called Earth was not just a result of random, fortunate, sequences of events.

They flew over the first range of mountains into a flat Salt Lake plain between. It had firing lanes full of targets of various sizes. The team was aligning for practice runs when their coms came to life.

"Phoenix Leader, Phoenix Leader, Phoenix Nest is under attack. I repeat, Phoenix Nest is under attack."

"Shit! Looks like we are baptizing these craft by fire. Fall into formation! Let's take those mother fuckers out!" Herrera called out to her squad.

"Phoenix Leader to Phoenix Nest. Are we going to have any additional air support? Over?"

"Roger, attempting to get fighters up as quickly as we can. Already taking casualties. Bravo and Charlie teams are airborne. Repeat copy, over?"

"Roger, Bravo and Charlie are airborne, thirty seconds to intercept."

Herrera's body tensed as the dog fight began to unfold in front of her.

"Bravo, Charlie, SITREP?" Herrera sent out on the commlinks.

"Glad you could rejoin, Alpha, or sorry, 'Phoenix,' now," the captain of Charlie answered back.

"What's the game plan?" Herrera asked.

"We don't have one," Bravo team leader shouted back. "We are severely outnumbered."

"Phoenix Leader to Phoenix Nest; do we have any more Phoenix Defenders ready to fly?"

Chief Saxum got on the headset. "We do, we just don't have anyone to fly them. So far, our ground troops are keeping their ground troops back for now. They are pummeling us with artillery, though. I don't know how much longer we can hold them."

"Bravo, Charlie, focus on the artillery and ground troops. Pull their cruisers over their heads. Maybe we can get lucky and have their stray fire work to our advantage."

"What are you going to do?" Bravo Leader asked.

"Try to keep them off your ass as best we can. Phoenix, take them out!"

"It's like a swarm of bees out here," Ferox shouted.

"How are they controlling so many of them?" Probus asked. "We saw that hangar; there is no way they have enough controllers to handle all of them."

"What are you thinking, Probus?" Pares asked.

"They must have them on some sort of tandem command code. Everyone, look out for patterns in their flight. If we can find a pattern, then we can divide them out."

"You heard her," Herrera called out. "Great work, Probus."

"Phoenix Nest, this is Phoenix Leader. What is the status on our artillery, over?'

"We are two units down. Refitting the remaining units. First volley in five minutes."

"This thing will be over in three minutes if we don't get some support. What is the status of our infantry?"

"Stepping out now."

"Roger, out," Herrera shouted through the intercom. "All right, boys, we are it for now."

"We won't be for long," Charlie Leader shouted. "I've lost two."

"Bravo lost one already, as well."

"It's time to go invisible," Herrera replied. "It will take them a few minutes to figure out what we've done. That should buy us some time to take out their artillery."

The confusion from Imperium was immediate as their return fire ceased while they figured out what had happened.

"Charlie, take out those cannons. Bravo, take out as many cruisers as you can. Phoenix team, let's do some work on their command truck."

CAPITULUM XXIII
(CHAPTER 23)

"Sir, we've lost visual." one of the Imperium controllers yelled out to Colonel Sectator.

Sectator looked up at the monitors. "Rewind the footage to right before you lost visual. I figure they have turned on their cloaking devices," he said as he reviewed the video. "Lock on their heat signatures. We can track and target them that way."

"Colonel! Status report!" Depravo shouted over the intercom. "They've taken out all but one of our artillery units. The Command Center is taking unidentified fire. What the fuck are you doing?"

"Sorry, sir, their aircraft turned on their cloaking devices. We are now targeting their heat signatures. We will be able to defend your position better in a few more minutes."

"Make it happen, Colonel. Now!"

Chief Saxum ordered the evacuation of LAX. Part of the old underground tunnel system led north to an old marina. Once all bystanders and non-critical personnel had evacuated, he would seal the tunnel for their protection.

Chief Saxum got on the Initium Novum emergency line to the stronghold in Wisconsin to update them on their situation and request backup.

"How can we help, Chief?"

"I need you to take out their hangar. Inside is the control system for their new aircraft. We take out the control, we take out the aircraft. We cannot afford to lose any of our craft, as we are using everything to defend our position. We are losing ground. We need this done ASAP," Chief Saxum replied.

"Roger, we are limited in craft and personnel but will not fail."

"I'm going to patch you into our asset, Alex Bellator. He is currently helping defend our position and has extensive knowledge of the grounds where the control center is located. Stand by."

The chief got back on the radio to the Phoenix team flying above. "Alex, this is the chief, over?"

"Hey, Chief, sure could use some help up here."

"I'm patching in the commanding officer from our Wisconsin stronghold. He needs the ins and outs of the Imperium compound."

"Um, little busy up here, Chief."

"They are going to take out the control center for those cruisers, so unless you want to take your chances, I would suggest talking to him."

"Patch him through." The dog fight continued above LAX as Alex shared his knowledge of the compound with the officer.

Charlie team was able to take out their artillery before Imperium was able to track their heat signature. The thick armor plating of the command center absorbed the rounds fired from their ships well enough to withstand the hits to its outer shell. Its anti-airstrike defense kept the Initium Novum's artillery from landing anywhere around it.

Imperium's ground forces began spreading out to the left and right, trying to find vulnerable points in the LAX compound's defenses.

"Chief! They are flanking to our north and south," one of the radar technicians shouted out.

The chief belted out his order to the communications team. "Shift artillery fire to push their advancements to the coastline on each side. Use our infantry to further divide both flanking forces and cut them off from their command center. Keep them pinned down on the coastline." He added, "Squadron leaders, provide cover for the infantry as they attempt to further divide their elements."

"Sir, they just took out our northern artillery unit."

"Shit! We can't hold them without it. What's the status of our birds?"

"Charlie is down to two, Bravo has four, Phoenix still has its whole unit."

"Herrera, it's the chief. I need you to refit Charlie with one of yours. Charlie, you hold their northern unit to the shoreline. Bravo, you cover the air overhead.

Phoenix, find a way to take out that damn command center," the chief commanded.

"Ferox, fall under Charlie, help them with the northern unit. Alex! Go take out the control center," Herrera ordered.

Ferox diverted himself to help Charlie squad.

Alex replied, "That's what we have been trying to do. The armor is too strong."

"No, Alex, I mean the main control center, at Imperium."

"What? Are you crazy? I can't leave."

"That's an order!" Herrera shouted.

"I'm not your soldier!" Alex shouted back.

"Alex…please." Herrera's voice softened as she continued. "The Wisconsin stronghold does not have a large enough unit to take out that hangar. It is the only hope we have at stopping these drones. We can't keep holding them like this for long. Taking out their aircraft is the only way we have a chance at defeating Imperium. Please, Alex, go!"

"I agree, Alex," Pares chimed in. "You know that place better than any of us."

Alex looked around at the swarm of angry aircraft around him. He looked below to the ground battle beneath. He knew they were right. "All right, got it."

Alex disengaged from the fight and pushed the craft supersonic. "Chief, patch me into the stronghold's attacking force. We need to come up with a game plan." Alex shot off like a rocket to the east.

"Sir! They are cutting off our northern and southern elements," one of the controllers yelled out to General Depravo.

"Colonel! Divert two squadrons to each northern and southern element. Have two defend the command post and four on the offensive," Depravo radioed to Sectator.

"Sir, we've taken out their last artillery unit."

"Excellent! It is just a matter of time before they fold. Advance our ground troops. Have our two flanking elements close inward. It is time to bring this to an end." Depravo laughed as sat back in his command chair watching the show in front of him.

• ────────── •

The chief began pacing in the war room as the last of their artillery was taken out. "Okay, Bravo, you take the southern element. Phoenix, defend the air above."

"Chief, the civilians have all safely evacuated. We can fight another day. We are losing ground. They are about to punch through our walls. Should we not evacuate?" Herrera asked.

"Negative, Herrera. If we evacuate through the tunnel, they will follow. We cannot outrun them. Our back is to the ocean, and they are closing in on all three sides. This is it. This is our last stand. Let's make it count."

"You heard him, boys," Herrera shouted on the radio. "We have nothing to lose. Let's go out with a bang."

Cheers and chants exploded over their headsets as they all pumped out one last adrenaline burst.

"It's all up to you," Herrera said under her breath as she closed her eyes for a moment to think of Alex. She opened her eyes and aggressively went on an offensive rage.

———————

Alex slowed his craft and dropped down to about a hundred feet above the ground. He followed the nap of the Earth along the highway leading to the front entrance of the Imperium compound. With his cloaking device and low altitude, he was hoping he was close enough to the ground to fly under its radar and undetectable to the human eye. He opened his com for one last radio transmission to the attacking unit of soldiers. "Wait for my signal. Then unleash hell."

"What is your signal?" the attacking unit's commanding officer asked.

"You'll know." Alex increased his speed and pulled the front gate up on his targeting display. "Here goes nothing."

A burst of fire appeared out of thin air, blowing the gate wide open. Alex pulled back on the yoke to a near ninety-degree incline, soaring straight up into the sky. From the wood line surrounding the compound, a thunderous burst of fire pelted its exterior.

The jolt of the gate exploding, and gunfire startled the crew in the hangar. "Sir! We're under attack. We are surrounded," shouted a junior officer to Sectator over the intercom.

"Stay on task," Sectator ordered to the drone controllers as he peered outside the hangar door. "Secure the perimeter," Sectator ordered. "What is the status of our front gate?"

"Fire came out of nowhere, Sir! Out of thin air."

"Shit!" Sectator said. "Pull up radar, look for heat signatures in the sky. We have unknown aircraft. Lock on those aircraft and blow them out of the sky."

Alex completed a full loop once he was out of range from any ground fire. Scrolling through his display options, he pulled up the coordinates of the hangar housing the drone controls. He knew as soon as he was in range of their antiaircraft systems he would be in trouble. He assumed they had already figured out what had happened and did not want to give them more time to prepare. He pushed the yoke forward and began his descent on the compound.

He pulled up the hangar on his targeting system as he descended onto the compound. He hoped he would be able to get off several well-aimed shots before being detected.

Suddenly alarms went off in his cockpit. Something had locked onto him. He looked around to see two Imperium cruisers coming up behind him. "Shit!" Alex knew he did not have time to take them both on. He knew they would get a shot off before he had time to do much of anything.

He pulled the trigger, firing several rounds at the hangar. As the impact alarm went off. Two rounds overshot as he quickly banked left before impact. The third hit him in his propulsion system, shutting the engine down and melting his two rear ailerons simultaneously.

He was in an uncontrollable nosedive without propulsion, and not on target. Time seemed to slow down as he watched Imperium's anti-airstrike system successfully take out the rounds he had fired as he was falling from the sky.

He thought about the team, about his family, about Herrera. He couldn't let them down. He had to figure out something. He couldn't let it end this way. He switched on the emergency orb transformation.

The ship began to deconstruct around him as he plummeted toward Earth. As his body became free from the craft, he struggled to hold onto the yoke. His legs began to flail as his body started tumbling out of control.

Alex pulled the heap of tangled mess into his chest. The transformation was not fully successful because of the damage it had sustained. He relaxed and straightened his legs and rolled over facing downward. The compound was coming into view as he was less than a few thousand feet from the ground. He aimed his body the best he could toward the hangar. He had only one shot at this and needed to make it count. He had only a matter of seconds before he would be a large blood spot on the concrete.

The mess of material vibrated and spattered its way back to life after Alex had initiated flight mode. "Come on, come on, you piece of shit." Adrenaline rushed through his veins as the ground grew close and closer.

He needed it to be fully formed to save his life. The safety system would not engage unless the craft was fully formed. He was hopeful he could get one burst of propulsion before it went back offline. It would be just enough to crash into the hangar and take out the control center.

His finger nervously tapped the accelerator while the craft was taking form. The concrete looked close enough to touch as "transformation complete" was heard in the cockpit. Alex let out an eager roar as he hit the accelerator one more time.

CAPITULUM XXIV
(CHAPTER 24)

"Sir! The connection between control and the aircraft has been severed," one of the controllers yelled out to Depravo.

"What? How? What's happening?" Depravo looked at the radar screen, then opened the door to the mobile command unit to look overhead. The remaining cruisers were changing course to return to the hangar. "Why are they changing course? Why are they not following the last command given?" Depravo became increasingly angry and anxious.

"It is an auto safeguard, sir. To protect the ship and pilot, there is an automatic return-to-base function installed in the software, should the connection to the server be cut."

"No! Shit! Can we reroute and reconnect from here?" Depravo asked nervously.

"I can try, sir."

"Get on it! Depravo got onto the radio. "Sectator! Status report. Sectator, status report! *Answer the God damned phone, Colonel!*"

•————————•

"Phoenix Nest, this is Phoenix Leader. We are seeing a drastic change in the enemy aircraft's flight pattern. Copy radar confirmation, over."

"Roger, Herrera," Saxum replied. "It looks as though all the aircraft are returning to their place of origin."

"Any indication that this is some type of diversion?"

"Negative. All indications show an exact reverse flight pattern from attack. Their pattern changed directly after we lost radio coms with Alex."

A mix of emotions flooded Herrera. She was excited that he accomplished what she knew he could. She was scared at the phrase "lost radio coms." She had to push it aside for now and focus on her mission.

"We have fire superiority; Phoenix crews support the infantry on the ground. Force a surrender from Imperium ground forces while we have the upper hand." The chief looked at his junior officer. "Get me a security detail. I want to personally invite that sick son of a bitch to surrender. Get the officer in charge of the offensive on the line. I want a status update."

The junior officer sent out the orders and got the officer on the line. "Chief, we are not making much headway after the defender crashed into the hangar. It is still well guarded. Would like to breach the front gate and requesting air support prior to breach, over."

"Roger, air support will be available in five minutes. Any word from our boy?"

"Negative, Chief. It was a spectacle to say the least. He crashed into the hangar from high altitude after taking a hit from two cruisers. Life expectancy from our vantage point is low, Chief."

"Roger, continue mission, out." The chief switched to the Phoenix squadrons above. "Herrera, how are we looking?"

"Ground forces have been successfully cut off from the control module. Charlie and Bravo are rounding up the southern forces while Alpha has the northern troops. Their surrender is inevitable. Any update on Alex?"

"Negative, Herrera. He sacrificed himself and his plane to take the cruiser control hangar out."

Deafening silence filled the air as the chief's words resonated with the squad. Herrera finally uttered, "Roger," understanding that his chance for survival was slim.

Both northern and southern attacking ground forces surrendered after their cruisers left and they lost their air support. Cheers from Initium Novum soldiers could be heard reverberating across the airfield as they brought in the Imperium soldiers.

Chief Saxum ordered the Phoenix squadrons to head to the Imperium compound for air support. Medical evacuation craft were on standby once the compound had been secured.

The chief's junior officer assembled crews for five armored vehicles to convoy out to the Imperium mobile command center of General Depravo to demand his surrender.

"Alex, this is Herrera. Do you copy?

Grief-filled and frustrated, Herrera shouted into her headset. *"Alex…Alex! Answer me, damn it!"*

"He's not going to answer," Pares said in a soft, calm tone. "It is time to focus on the rest of our mission, ma'am. We need to secure the compound, and then we can worry about recovery." A few seconds of silence passed before Pares continued. "I'm sorry, ma'am. He did what he had to do. Any of us would've done the same thing. It's time to focus, ma'am"

Herrera fought back tears as she listened to her most trusted advisor. He was right. She had to put those feelings aside and continue the mission. She hated Alex for falling for him. She hated that the one man she was able to open to, she sent on a suicide mission. She hated herself for getting attached.

"Roger, Pares. Take Ferox and provide cover for the Western offensive. Probus and I will take the east. Charlie and Bravo, cover the main entrance and antiaircraft defense systems."

With the control hangar destroyed, the Phoenix squads had no trouble taking out the guard towers and antiaircraft systems. Within a matter of minutes Initium Novum had the compound secured and remaining Imperium soldiers surrendered.

Herrera radioed LAX. "Send the medevac. Compound secured."

———————————————

"Sir, our ground troops have surrendered. Headquarters is under attack and is about to fold. What do we do, sir?"

An anxious Imperium soldier looked to General Depravo sitting in his chair in the command center. There were three controllers at their stations, all looking for guidance and direction, all hoping there was some miracle Depravo had left.

"Do you feel like dying today?" asked General Depravo in a smug, sarcastic tone.

The three soldiers all shook their heads.

"Then I guess the only thing left for you to do, is… surrender."

The three looked at each other, confused, then to General Depravo. "Go on, you're dismissed. Go surrender."

The three slowly stood up. One asked, "Aren't you coming, sir?"

Depravo reclined in his chair and crossed his legs. He studied their bewildered faces for a moment, put on his gloves, then stood up. "Gentlemen, I am the commander of the Imperium Army. I am *the* ruler." He slowly walked toward them. "You three are my last line of defense. Are you really going to let the enemy take your leader? Do you really want the fall of Imperium on your shoulders?"

"No, sir, we just thought—"

General Depravo put his hand on the shoulder of the soldier. "That's the problem, isn't it? That is *always* the problem. Let me help with that." Depravo raised his free hand and pressed his thumb into the soldier's forehead. The black tar-like substance started running down his face.

Before the other two could react, he shoved the soldier out of his way and managed to smear the rest of the Black Death on both the remaining soldiers' foreheads. All three of them began to violently shake as the Black Death drained them of themselves.

Once their bodies stopped seizing, he ordered all of them to stand at attention. "I need a little distraction, and you three are going to provide it."

Chief Saxum's convoy rolled to a stop about fifty meters from the Imperium command unit. The chief dismounted his vehicle and got on the megaphone. "This is Chief Saxum of Initium Novum. You are surrounded. Your troops have surrendered. Slowly exit your post with your hands raised."

The door to the command unit opened and three soldiers slowly walked down the stairs and lined up, side by side, facing the convoy.

"Drop your weapons and raise your hands," the chief yelled into the megaphone.

The soldiers stood motionless, emotionless, side arms in hand, at their sides.

"Drop your weapons and raise your hands," the chief repeated.

Initium Novum soldiers all had their weapons drawn on the three, waiting for the slightest sign of compliance.

Simultaneously the three slowly raised their firearms. Within a second multiple rounds penetrated their bodies as the Initium Novum soldiers opened fire.

A small squad raced up to the bodies, weapons drawn, to investigate. A loud boom came from the command trailer as a pod shot up into the sky. It quickly morphed into a cruiser and shot off into the distance before the convoy had time to react.

The convoy of soldiers did a quick sweep of the abandoned command unit, only to find Depravo's gloves lying on the floor. The chief let out a frustrated yell as he realized Depravo had escaped.

CAPITULUM XXV
(CHAPTER 25)

Herrera and her squadron landed their planes as the ground troops rounded up the rest of the Imperium soldiers.

"Bravo, Charlie, release the prisoners. Alpha, on me, let's go look for Alex."

"Ma'am, if I could—" Pares began.

"No, you cannot," Herrera snapped. "Move out."

Bravo and Charlie squadrons departed toward the cell blocks. Herrera and her team raced toward the hangar.

The hangar door had been blown inward, and part of the roof had collapsed. Random electrical sparks could be seen through the rubble as they reached the outside of the hangar door.

Pares said to Ferox and Probus, "Watch out for exposed wires. Keep a lookout for any sign of movement. This building is unstable. Be prepared for a fast egress if it starts coming down."

The back of Alex's ship could be seen under the rubble of knocked-over cabinets and shelves. His flight path was clear. He burst through the hangar door straight through the control panel, knocking three of the pod clusters out on his path into the hangar office, where he finally stopped.

Light fixtures and pieces of drop-down ceiling dangled from above the wreckage. Body parts of the control panel crew were smeared along the path like a deer hit by a semitruck.

"What do you think the last thing was that went through their heads?" asked Probus.

"The plane," joked ferox as stepped over smeared blood.

"Shut up!" Probus shot back at Ferox as he gave a pirate's smile.

"Be careful removing things from around the ship. I don't want a cave-in while we are trying to recover him," Herrera ordered.

The team slowly uncovered the defender Alex was flying. A hand emerged from the rubble at the front of the ship. Then an arm. Ferox brushed the dust aside to read his nametag. "Sectator. Remind me not to challenge Alex to darts, 'cause this was a bullseye."

"Ferox!" Pares yelled.

Ferox looked around at the faces of the team, realizing he had made a careless remark. "Sorry, I…sorry." Ferox continued to remove the debris from Sectator and the nose of the plane while the rest of the crew attempted to free the cockpit.

As Ferox went to check for a pulse on Sectator, he felt the cold nose of a firearm at his temple. "Uh, guys?" Ferox muttered.

Sectator had managed to free his hand, secure his firearm, and press it against Ferox's head.

The rest of the team dropped what they were doing and raised their own firearms toward Sectator.

"We can stay like this until you bleed out or you can drop your weapon," Pares said to Sectator.

His arm was weak, and he could barely lift his head to meet the eyes of the team staring him down. "You'll never defeat him," Sectator was able to murmur. "I might as well take one of you with me."

Without flinching Pares fired and hit Sectator square in the forehead. Blood spattered on the side of Ferox's face.

"Fuck, Pares!" Ferox said, wiping his face "Give me a fucking heart attack."

"You're welcome." Pares snarked. "Now let's try to open this cockpit.

"The emergency release is not responding," said Probus as she pressed the emergency release on the outside of the ship.

Through the wreckage the team was able to find a few pieces of rebar to jam into the aircraft to open the hatch. After several tries the team was able to convince the hatch to break free. They worked together to carefully remove the top to expose the cockpit. To all of their surprise, it was empty.

"I don't understand." Herrera looked at Pares. "How can this be?"

"He must have ejected," Pares answered.

"But how? The ground troops did not report seeing a parachute."

"Unless he did so at the last minute and the parachute never had time to deploy."

Herrera's eye widened. "Check the perimeter, all around this hangar. Look of a chute, anything that may locate him. Now!"

The team spread out, sorting through rubbish, looking for Alex. Herrera walked around the exterior of the building. She stared at the impact site and tried to envision what an ejection would look like. She followed the building around to the back side, where there was a large trash bin.

"No way," she said to herself as she climbed up the exterior ladder. She peered over the ledge to see Alex wearily holding his firearm in her direction. When he saw her, his arm dropped like a sandbag at his side.

Herrera climbed over the edge of the dumpster and stumbled through the trash to his side. He had superficial cuts and scrapes on his extremities, face, and chest. He had shrapnel sticking out of his left leg and arm.

"You've lost a lot of blood," Herrera said to Alex. "Are you able to stand?"

"I think my legs are broken." Alex groaned.

Herrera got on her radio. "We need a medic to the rear of the operations hangar in the dumpster, now!"

"Repeat that? Over," replied a man over the radio.

"This is Captain Herrera, and I need a God damn medic to the dumpster at the rear of the operations hanger, *now*!"

"Roger, ma'am. Medics on the way."

"We do it?" Alex asked.

"Yes, we did. You did. You saved us," Herrera said, fighting back tears.

Alex nodded with a slight smile. "I'm glad I got to see you." He stared into Herrera's tear-filled eyes as the world around him became burry and dark.

"Stay with me, Alex. Stay with me. Alex! *Medic!*"

The slow, steady beep of a heart monitor counted the time away as Herrera sat at Alex's bedside. It had been two days since the battle ended. The Imperium forces had surrendered, and their prisoners set free.

The top leaders Depravo had imprisoned were transferred to Initium Novum's lockup to await sentencing for war crimes. No word had come concerning Depravo's whereabouts since his escape.

Herrera sat with her elbows on her knees, her hands clasped under her chin, watching, waiting for any sign of life from Alex.

While Alex was unconscious, he underwent several surgeries to repair the damage from his wreck. The fragments had successfully been removed and his legs put in traction and casted. Doctors had placed him in a medically induced coma to handle all the medical procedures safely.

She sat patiently waiting for the medications to wear off and for him to regain consciousness. She studied his bruised and battered face. As fearful as she was that he may never awaken, she was also in awe of how truly remarkable he was.

Alex had endured so much pain and sacrifice in his life. He survived two plane crashes, multiple tortures, and a death-defying escape from a prison in the short time she has known him.

Chief Saxum, Pares, Probus, and Ferox interrupted her thoughts when they came into his room.

"You need to take a break, Herrera," the chief said. "You've been here for two days. Go take a shower, get some grub, and take a break."

"Chief, I—"

"That's an order, Herrera. We got him. One of us will sit with him. Go."

Herrera reluctantly stood up. She stretched her arms over her head and let out a yawn. "I'll be back," she said to Alex as she squeezed his hand and gave him a kiss on the forehead.

Her grip released and she turned to leave the room. Alex's fingers twitched and then grabbed her hand before it left his reach.

"Fucking hell?" Alex groaned as he regained consciousness.

"Easy, Alex. You're okay. We are all here." Herrera leaned over and brushed his hair and the side of his face with her free hand.

Alex let out a few more groans as he tried to adjust himself in the bed. "What the fuck happened?"

"You passed out from blood loss. We used medevac to get you back here to LAX. You have two broken legs in traction. Large metal shrapnel was removed from your left thigh and bicep."

"Dude! You've got tell me how you ended up in the dumpster," Ferox blurted out. The chief shot him a glare. "Sorry, Chief."

Herrera helped Alex to sit up a little. He cleared his throat. "The two cruisers were on my tail. They hit me, and I lost power. I thought maybe if I shut it down and booted it back up, maybe I could get the engines to fire.

"The ship reformed, and at the last second the engine fired, and I shot straight toward the hangar, a few feet from the ground. I thought I had a better chance of survival if I punched out. I lined the ship up and ejected. My seat back hit the roof and I tumbled like a rag doll across the roof and off into the dumpster."

"You are one lucky son of a bitch," Pares remarked.

"What now?" asked Alex.

"You are going to recover. Imperium is done. We will slowly rebuild and bring some peace back to the world. The war is over," the chief replied.

"Depravo?"

"Unfortunately, he escaped. There has been no trace of him yet. One by one we are shutting down all the remaining Imperium bases and facilities. He has nowhere to go. We will find him eventually."

"Then the war is not over, just paused," said Alex.

"He is without resources, he has nowhere to go. If he shows his ugly head, we will be ready."

"Let's hope so, for everyone's sake. In the meantime,…" Alex looked over the Herrera and motioned her toward him. He reached up to brush the hair out of her face.

She leaned into the warmth of his hand as he rested it on her cheek. The pair exchanged smiles, and she leaned over the bed.

"You both realize we are all still in the room, right?" Ferox interrupted. "Not like you can do much there, Alex."

"Shut up, Ferox," Herrera said as she leaned over Alex for a soft, warm, passion-filled kiss.

EPILOGUE

As the weeks went by, Initium Novum began cleanup operations. To ration out food, clothing, and shelter, a census was taken of all the prisoners held against their will. The wounded, ill, and malnourished were treated.

The war criminals were tried and sentenced. All the salvageable technology was secured and the formula for Black Death destroyed. Their buildings were transitioned into temporary housing while residential records could be reviewed, and people felt safe returning to family homes.

The supply operations that had been established through Imperium were restored to help spread resources. Jobs were created to rebuild and refurbish cities and towns across the world.

Sheriffs were placed in each small colony to continue safety and protection from would-be criminals. Officials were elected to rewrite policies and laws to return order and structure. The financial resources of Imperium were distributed evenly by population density. Hope flourished as work and education resumed.

Alex became fully rehabilitated and rejoined the team as it provided guidance and oversight on the restorations. Chief Saxum was promoted to the secretary of the armed forces. Pares retired and was elected to office as a state senator. Herrera and Alex began to build their life together. Alex knew who he was and where he belonged.

The steady sound of water dripping down inside the dark cavern was mind numbing. Depravo had been inside the top-secret Imperium base for months with a small crew of Imperium troops.

It was the last remaining outpost. Depravo's aircraft had just enough power to get him here. They were in the northernmost point in what used to be Alaska. They had been trapped in the cave for weeks because of the winter weather.

Depravo pulled out a small vial from his pocket. He shook it around and stared at it as it settled. Soon he would have his revenge.